STEVE HEUZINKVELD

SURVIVORS OF THE FALL

THE FALL SERIES BOOK ONE

First published by Steve Heuzinkveld 2022

Copyright © 2022 by Steve Heuzinkveld

All rights reserved. No part of this publication may be reproduced, stored or transmitted in any form or by any means, electronic, mechanical, photocopying, recording, scanning, or otherwise without written permission from the publisher. It is illegal to copy this book, post it to a website, or distribute it by any other means without permission.

This novel is entirely a work of fiction. The names, characters and incidents portrayed in it are the work of the author's imagination. Any resemblance to actual persons, living or dead, events or localities is entirely coincidental.

Steve Heuzinkveld asserts the moral right to be identified as the author of this work.

First edition

ISBN: 978-0-6452886-3-6

This book was professionally typeset on Reedsy.
Find out more at reedsy.com

Dedicated to my wife, Hariezoy,
the strongest woman I know.

Foreword

While this story is based on real locations throughout the United States, I have used fictitious names for some towns and neighborhoods, so that I can change certain aspects of these locations for the sake of the story.

Thank you, and enjoy!

CHAPTER 1

Riley Armstrong should have known that something was wrong when she saw her father striding across the front yard, still wearing his police uniform.

He preferred to keep his occupation a secret among all of their neighbors – always showering and changing into regular clothes at the station after his shift, and parking their family's red suburban in the garage, so that nobody would pass by and see his police gear in the backseat.

But today, the car was sitting in the driveway, and it was barely ten in the morning.

"What did you forget?" Riley smirked at him as she opened the screen door.

"Where's your mother?" Nolan Armstrong's stubbled jaw was set firmly as he bounded up the veranda's stairs two at a time, fists clenching and unclenching.

"Sounds like she's in the kitchen," she shrugged, nodding down the hall towards the chorus of banging cupboards.

"Why aren't you dressed?" he frowned as his eyes adjusted in the shade underneath the veranda.

"Dad, you've seen me wearing this before," she glanced down

1

at her white crop top and denim mini shorts, knowing that he hadn't.

"Go upstairs and change," he said bluntly, punching the screen door against the stucco wall and pushing past Riley.

"But I'm..." she paused to look back at her father, massaging her shoulder, wondering what had gotten into him.

He had never been so aggressive towards her in the past.

Something was definitely off today.

The screen door swung shut behind her, as if prompting her to just brush it off.

"I'm going out," she continued, her tone tauter. "Calvin's gonna be here any second."

"Calvin..?" Nolan stopped halfway down the hall and put his hands on his hips, his police kit belt rustling as he turned back around, narrowing his eyes at his daughter.

"You've met Calvin, at graduation," Riley's eyebrows furrowed. She cocked her head slightly. Granted, today was only their second date, but her father knew every boy who had ever shown an interest in her, to the point that she was convinced that he had conducted background checks on all of them. She glanced back at the street before asking, "Dad, is everything okay?"

"Everything is..." Nolan held up a hand, as if he was about to explain something to her, but he trailed off halfway, his gaze sliding sideways towards the study. He stroked the stubble across his jaw and raised his eyebrows at Riley. "You're not going out."

"We're just going for brunch at the marina," she opened the screen door halfway, wishing that Calvin's car would just turn the corner already so that she could make her escape. "It's not a big deal. I'll be home before dinner."

"No, you're not going anywhere," he maintained with a troubling tinge in his tone, taking a step towards her. "Whatever plans you've made, cancel them."

"Ugh, fine, I'll get changed," Riley let the screen door swing shut behind her as she trudged towards the staircase.

She had her foot on the first step when a blue sedan's horn honked twice outside.

Perfect timing, she thought to herself.

Well, almost.

Perfect timing would have been five minutes ago.

"Oh, that's him!" she exclaimed, whirling away from the staircase, "Later, Dad!"

His hand caught hold of her wrist before she could reach the door.

For a man in his mid-forties, her father's reactions were still lightning fast – a boon in his profession, and a bane in her adolescence.

"Dad, let go," Riley grimaced, her shoulder rising involuntarily as his grip tightened. "You're hurting me!"

Being a policeman's daughter had its benefits. Instinctively, she turned her palm downwards so that her thumb was in line with his, and then pushed out with her elbow, breaking the hold.

Nolan anticipated the move.

After all, he had taught it to her.

With a metallic jingle, his other hand shot out from behind his hip, clapping a handcuff around her wrist.

"What the *hell!?*" the rest of Riley's repertoire of self defense techniques crumbled in the cold embrace of his handcuffs, the steel fangs snapping shut, tight enough to bite into her skin.

"I'm serious," an unfamiliar tone menaced through her

father's gritted teeth as he swung her arm back towards the staircase, fastening the other end of the handcuffs to the metal railing. "From now on, you do exactly what I say, when I say it. Clear?"

CHAPTER 2

"Are you freaking kidding me!?" Riley raged, wrenching at the handcuffs and screaming in frustration as the shackle's edge dug into her wrist.

Part of her wanted to believe that her father was thrusting her into an uncomfortable situation just to gauge her reaction.

Not every attacker fought fairly, and she had to be ready for the world.

She knew that it was part of his responsibility as a parent to be overprotective of her, but this was too much.

Any second now, he would unlock the handcuffs and give her the same old lecture on how important it was for her to keep her guard up, at all times. Maybe then he would teach her how to slip her hand out of the cuffs, or even share some top secret police technique on how to pop the lock open without the key.

The other part of her offered a different explanation, but she forced it out of her mind.

That wasn't going to happen to her.

Not her father.

Not her family.

"Alright, you've made your point," Riley swallowed her

uncertainty, glancing sidelong at her father with a resigned expression.

She leaned her hip and shoulder against the railing with a small snort, wondering how stupid she must have looked in front of him, trying to pull metal through metal.

He wasn't laughing though.

He didn't even smile.

"I'll talk to Calvin," was all he gave her, turning towards the screen door.

"Wait, what?" Riley's confusion fell on deaf ears as the door bounced off the stucco wall with a rattle and swung back into the latch, her father marching down the garden path.

A feeling of unease began to spread from Riley's gut, traveling in cold fingers up her spine, tainting her thoughts.

Nolan Armstrong had been a police officer for over two decades. In all of those years, he had never raised a hand to Riley or her mother – not even showing a hint of aggression.

But she knew that not all police families had a happy ending. The daily dangers that they faced. The horrible things they saw people do to each other. Putting their lives and sanity on the line each and every day and then coming home to pretend that it was all just another regular day at work so that they wouldn't have to talk about it.

Riley's pupils dilated.

Maybe today was the day that he finally snapped.

And she was caught like a rabbit in a snare.

She stared in horror as her father leaned down into Calvin's car window, one hand resting on the hilt of his holstered service pistol.

"Mom?" she called over the sounds of rustling coming from the kitchen.

No answer.

Just more cupboards slamming.

"Mom – Dad just cuffed me to the stairs," she strained at her restraints in vain before glancing outside again. Her father was unbuttoning the strap on his holster. "Mom!!"

"Do as your father says," Susan Armstrong's voice floated from the kitchen, quiet and mechanical. Silence hung in the air for a moment before the sounds of rustling and rummaging continued.

"Are you seriously cooking right now!?" Riley started hyperventilating.

This wasn't happening.

She was dreaming.

She had to be.

Or she had woken up in the wrong house.

Calvin's tires screeched as his blue sedan peeled off down the street.

Nolan Armstrong – or whoever had stolen his body – strode back up the garden path.

Heaving shallow breaths, stars exploded across Riley's retinas and her vision began to blur, with pins and needles prickling her hands and feet.

She didn't even realize that her father was already back inside the house until his callused hand closed around the lower half of her face.

CHAPTER 3

"Breathe," Nolan Armstrong tilted Riley's head back with a no-nonsense expression on his face.

He was holding his hand over her mouth, while his forefinger pressed one of her nostrils shut. She turned her head and smacked his wrist to the side with her free arm.

"It's kinda hard to breathe with your –" her panting indignation was cut short as he closed his hand around her mouth again.

"Breathe," he repeated, his tone stern as ever, "And then we'll talk."

Riley could only imagine how much worse he was with the criminals that he caught breaking the law. He was a sinewy man, strong enough to restrain someone by physical force alone, but she supposed that he had to be.

She glared back at him in disdain. She might have been more tolerant of his hand over her face if his eyebrows weren't raised in that patronizing way that she always hated.

He could shut her mouth, but not her eyes.

If looks could kill, Riley would have been half an orphan, even though she was already eighteen years old.

Even so, she could feel a weight beginning to lift from her chest with every deep breath, and the blurred edges of her vision were straightening out again.

Having stared enough daggers at her father, Riley glanced towards the closed and locked hardwood front door, cutting off the view to the street and the outside world.

Her mother's endless dumping of ingredients across the kitchen counter was magnified in the silence. Baking was something that Susan Armstrong did to manage her stress, instead of actually doing something about whatever was stressing her.

That got Riley wondering. *Did Mom know that he was gonna be like this when he got home?*

She batted her father's hand away a second time.

She was still breathing hotly, but now it was more out of defiance rather than dismay.

Nolan studied his daughter for a few stretched seconds before giving her a small nod, seemingly satisfied.

"Are you gonna uncuff me now?" Riley shook her shackle in contempt.

"In a minute," he spun on his boot heel, scuffing the hall's tiles as he disappeared into the study.

"At least tell me why you almost pulled a gun on Calvin," she called after him.

"I had to make sure he wasn't coming back," Nolan replied over the top of a series of high-pitched bleeps, "Can't have you climbing out the window."

Riley slumped against the staircase's railing, her shackled hand still dangling uselessly in the air. He knew her too well — one of the drawbacks of having a policeman for a father.

She didn't imagine that he had rushed home from work to stop her from going out on a harmless brunch date though.

Her ears pricked up as she heard the familiar routine of metallic rattles and slides emanating from the study – the telltale sounds of her father checking his preferred handgun. It normally never even left the room, but today was far from normal.

"Susan, you almost done in there?" he called down the hall as he emerged from the study, buttoning up the strap on his holster.

"I really don't know what I'm meant to be doing, Nolan," Susan answered, her drawn face appearing in the doorway. "Could you give me a hand?"

Just like Riley, Susan Armstrong was lithe and slender, with light brown hair. Sometimes, it felt as though she was staring into a mirror from the future.

"Can someone *please* just tell me what's going on!?" Riley fumed, her hazel eyes darting between the two.

Her parents exchanged a glance before her father fished into his police kit belt for the key to the handcuffs.

"What I'm about to tell you," Nolan leveled his gaze with hers. His stubbled jaw was still set firmly, but his tone had finally softened to a recognizable tone, "You can't tell anyone else. Understood?"

"Yeah, I guess," Riley shrugged, more relieved at the prospect of being freed rather than worrying about her own ability to keep a secret.

"Riley?" he tested, his eyebrows raised.

"Fine, yes," she stared pointedly at the key hovering above her wrist.

"We need to leave the city," he glanced sidelong at her mother standing in the doorway to the kitchen. Susan was gazing back at him with her arms folded, as if she needed to hear it again, straight from his mouth. He took a deep breath, still struggling to comprehend it himself. "There's an asteroid on a direct collision course for the West Coast."

CHAPTER 4

Riley Armstrong rubbed at the red ring around her wrist as she followed her parents into the kitchen. Scattered across the bench tops were boxes of cereal, cans of baked beans, jars of sandwich spreads, and packets of chips and crackers.

"I don't know if that's everything," Susan confessed, studying the remaining contents of their kitchen cupboards. "Unless you want what's in the fridge?"

"No, this is good," Nolan stroked his stubbled jaw before reconsidering. "Actually, we could probably go through the bread and the fruit while we're on the road. Riley, could you grab the picnic basket and a couple of buckets from the laundry? Riley?"

She was too busy browsing the internet on her phone, looking for a news article to support her father's outlandish claim. After all, he wasn't an astronomer – aside from the occasional stargaze while taking out the trash.

"Nobody's talking about an asteroid," Riley changed her search terms just to be certain, but she wasn't getting any results. She glanced up at her father with her eyebrows furrowed before crossing the room into the lounge, thumbing the TV remote and flicking through the news channels. "Nothing. Dad, are you sure about this?"

"No news is good news for us," he looked over at Susan, jerking his head towards the laundry, "The less people who know about it, the better."

"But it might not even exist," Riley cocked her head slightly, trying to see the purpose behind her father's concern. She clicked the TV off and rounded on him. "Is this why you almost pulled a gun on Calvin? Over a freaking rumor?"

"It's not a rumor," he turned his attention to the kitchen island, sorting the cereal boxes from the jars and cans. "The whole department got called in this morning. Even Keith was there."

"I thought Keith was suspended?" Susan bustled back into the kitchen with an armful of buckets.

"Not today," Nolan replied as he began packing the groceries. "Chief wants everyone on high alert for any signs of rioting and looting. He said that the asteroid's slated to hit the East Coast, but he wants to get ahead of the public before the media goes live with the story."

"But... we aren't on the East Coast," Riley frowned at her mother, who faltered with a can of baked beans. "Why do we need to leave the city?"

"Because that's not where the asteroid's going," Nolan explained as he tipped the contents of the fruit bowl into one of the buckets. "Keith and I got assigned to escort duty. The governor's bringing his whole family with him to the airport. Even his extended relatives. Call it coincidence, but I'm not taking that chance."

"People need to know," Riley held her phone in her hand, thinking about her friends.

13

"No, they don't," he raised his eyebrows at her. "Not until we're out of Redhurst."

"But everyone else should have a chance to prepare," she argued, her gaze shifting between her parents, shocked that they were even considering keeping this to themselves. "Think about how many people could die. How many *millions* of people."

"Think about how many cars will be on the roads," Susan countered, seeing the sense in maintaining their silence. "If word gets out too early, the freeways will get clogged up, and we'll never be able to leave."

Riley didn't say anything.

She didn't even know what to say.

The government and the media were working together to keep the public in the dark, making sure that they didn't panic prematurely.

It made perfect sense, and yet it all felt so wrong.

Countless lives were on the line, and everyone who knew about it was more than willing to make the sacrifice.

Including her parents.

"Riley, we just have to beat the traffic," her father crossed the room to take her by the shoulders, sensing the moral dilemma going through her mind. "As soon as we're out of the city, you can tell the whole world about it."

"It's just – it's..." she struggled to form the words.

"We don't have a lot of time," his stern tone returned as he rubbed his stubbled jaw and looked back at Susan. "Keith and I weren't the only ones on escort duty. And one of the governor's aides is probably wondering why he just cleared his whole schedule. Someone else is gonna figure it out. Every minute that we waste here is a risk that they'll leak it to the public, and we'll get caught up in the chaos."

"Come on, Riley, I'll help you pack," Susan offered, when a thought crossed her mind. She paused beside the knife block before picking out the biggest blade, dropping the kitchen knife in with the bucket of fruit.

CHAPTER 5

Riley Armstrong sat in the backseat of their red suburban as her father backed out of the driveway, staring out at their family home for what was most likely the last time she would ever see it again.

Granted, it wasn't the palatial estate that the privileged kids of Southern California had grown up in, but it was still the embodiment of all of her fondest childhood memories.

Riding her first bicycle down the quiet suburban street.

Running through the sprinkler on hot summer days.

Celebrating birthdays and holidays with barbecues in the backyard.

If her father's theory about the asteroid was correct, then those memories would be the only things that she would have left of her childhood. The old family photo albums were somewhere up in the attic, and they didn't have enough time to sort through the clutter.

"Wait!" Riley sat up in her seat just as her father shifted gears in the street.

"What did you forget?" Nolan sighed as he stared up at the rearview mirror.

Riley didn't answer him.

She only wound down the window and whipped out her phone, tilting it sideways to take a picture of their house.

"Okay," she sighed, stowing her phone back into her pocket.

Nolan and Susan shared a sympathetic glance, interlacing their fingers over the center console.

Riley stared over her shoulder until they turned the corner and their house dropped out of sight, her gaze soon falling to her lap. She had changed out of her previous ensemble, thinking that a pair of faded denim jeans and a green quarter-sleeve shirt might be more appropriate for getting out of the city.

"Where are we going?" she hadn't even thought to ask until now.

"Your grandmother's farm in Nebraska," Nolan answered unenthusiastically.

Riley knew that it was serious now, because she knew how much he loathed visiting her mother's relatives in Nebraska.

The long drive itself was reason enough, but her Aunt Lorraine would always needle at him to no end every time that they made the interstate trip, begrudging him for having stolen her sister away to California.

If there was one person who would welcome the news of an asteroid hitting the West Coast, it would be Aunt Lorraine.

"We have to make a stop first though," Nolan took his mind off the road trip ahead as they stopped at a set of traffic lights. He thumbed his phone's screen in the dashboard's cradle before settling back in the driver's seat to use the hands-free feature, "Dial Keith Bowman."

Keith was his partner on the police force. Riley remembered that their families would eat at restaurants together – at least once per week – up until a few years ago, when Keith's wife had filed for a divorce. The last thing that Riley had overheard about the man was that he had been serving a suspension for drinking on the job.

"Nolan! Almost good to go," Keith's whiskey-cured voice rang clear through the loudspeaker. "I'm on my way over to Palmview right now."

"Palmview?" Nolan echoed as the traffic lights turned green.

"Yeah, Jesse's not picking up his phone," Keith replied before cursing an apparently slow driver in front of him. "He's still living with Old Limp Dick and the Whore Queen."

"Keith, I've got my family in the car," Nolan said sheepishly as he glanced up at the rearview mirror to see Riley smirking out the window.

"Oh," an awkward silence hung in the air as Keith fumbled for a reply. "Hey, Susan, Riley. I've been stuttering lately. I meant to say Karen and Stuart. Yeah."

"Alright, we'll meet you there," Nolan cut the conversation short as he hung a left at the next intersection.

"You sure?" Keith asked, his truck's engine revving in the background, "Won't take me but a minute. I've already got all his sh– uh, things packed."

"We'll see you soon, Keith," Susan replied before ending the call, casting a sidelong stare at her husband. "How do you know where Karen's house is?"

"We just patrol the neighborhood every now and then," Nolan shrugged, gazing intently at the road ahead. "Anyway, I'm driving."

Riley stifled a smile at her parents as her phone buzzed in her pocket.

It was almost enough to take her mind off the asteroid that

was threatening to turn the West Coast into a giant crater.

Almost.

"Hey, sorry I had to take off earlier," a message from Calvin displayed across Riley's lock screen. "Your dad threatened to put holes in my car. He seemed like a nice guy at graduation. I don't understand what I did wrong."

Riley unlocked her phone and tapped on his message to reply, but she didn't know what to say to defend her father without telling Calvin about the asteroid.

"Maybe we can meet up later tonight?" Calvin persisted, despite her father's threats.

"Sorry, I can't," Riley's thumbs flew over the miniature keyboard, but she bit her bottom lip as she grasped for something else to show that she was still interested.

She couldn't exactly type, "Maybe next time," or, "Let's try again next week."

There was no next time at the marina.

For Calvin, there might not even be a next week.

Riley glanced outside the window at all of the other cars on the road. Ordinary people were just going about their weekend, visiting friends, dropping off deliveries, shopping for groceries. They had no idea what was about to happen.

"We have to leave Redhurst," she finally settled on, before adding, "You should too."

"WTF? Why?" his reply was almost instant.

She looked up at her father in the rearview mirror before staring down at her phone again, torn with indecision.

One person won't make a difference, a small voice in the back of her mind whispered.

"Asteroid incoming, government cover-up," she typed out, swallowing as her thumb hovered over the send button.

Just as Riley was about to delete the message, deciding to wait until later to respond, one of their wheels ran over a pothole on the road, and her phone bounced in her hand.

She shut her eyes, still unsure of which button she would have preferred to press.

Her eyelids snapped open again as her phone vibrated.

"Shit! Are you serious!?" Calvin shot back. "I'll text you later."

"Don't tell anyone else," Riley quickly added.

No reply.

CHAPTER 6

Palmview Beach was a stylish seaside suburb that was almost exclusively occupied by the upper middle class who could afford to live in its luxury ocean vista villas.

The Armstrong Family's red suburban seemed like an outcast among all of the stately sedans and convertible sports cars comprising the local traffic.

Riley was crestfallen as she stole glimpses of the ocean's cerulean canvas in the narrow side streets that led down towards the beach. She was supposed to have been eating brunch at the marina just on the other side of the row of regal residences, watching windsurfers and jet skis cutting swathes through the waves.

Instead, she was eating an apple in the backseat as they pulled up behind Keith Bowman's black crew cab pickup, similarly stacked with boxes and buckets of supplies for the road.

Classy as ever, Keith had mounted the curb and parked his truck on the verdant green grass of Karen and Stuart Sinclair's otherwise dignified front yard.

"What are you, drunk!?" Karen's shrill voice rang through the affluent neighborhood. "Get the hell off our lawn before I call the police!"

"Why bother calling?" Keith laughed derisively, holding his arms out wide in case she had missed his uniform, "I'm already here!"

"Is that Karen?" Susan peered out the passenger window, "She looks terrible."

It had been years since Riley had seen the Bowmans.

Keith looked exactly as she remembered him – broad-shouldered with close-cropped hair. But Karen was practically unrecognizable, apart from her voice. The woman was a skeletal beanpole now, with platinum blonde hair and an obvious set of implants.

"You don't deserve to wear that badge!" Karen spat, becoming increasingly aware that they were already beginning to draw a crowd.

An elderly neighbor doddered around the side of his house, gawking across the street as he hosed down his driveway, while a deliveryman whipped out his phone to capture the conflict. Farther down the street, a woman walking her Dachshund paused to let her dog get acquainted with a fire hydrant.

"Can't you just accept that Jesse's happier here with us?" Karen lowered her tone, forcing Riley to sidle closer to the open passenger window to catch the rest of their conversation. "He's not a kid anymore. If he wanted to go anywhere with you, he would actually talk to you. Don't you think it's odd that he never picks up the phone whenever you call?"

"I don't believe a word that comes outta your mouth," Keith fired back, pacing back and forth in front of the doorstep. He looked over his shoulder to see Riley's family parked beside his truck on the side of the road. Squaring up again, he asked, "Why don't you call him outside so he can say it to my face?"

"Do we really need to be here?" Riley asked her parents as Karen slammed the door and disappeared into the house. "We could've just met them on our way outta the city."

"We'll be on our way soon," Nolan glanced out the window, his police radio picking up chatter in the silence as he made eye contact with the elderly man across the street.

The neighbor shot back a look of disgust, as if driving a middle class suburban was a symptom of an infectious disease.

"Hope so," Riley bit into a crunchy chunk of her apple, chewing for a moment before adding, "When you said we needed to leave the West Coast, I didn't think we'd be starting *from* the coast."

"Get that pile of junk off my lawn!" an overweight silver-haired man dressed in a blue tracksuit burst out of the Sinclair house, holding a rolled-up newspaper aloft as if he was about to take a swing at Keith.

"You'd better think twice before you strike a police officer!" Nolan Armstrong jumped out of the suburban to back up his partner.

"What is this, the bum parade?" Stuart Sinclair fumed as Karen and Jesse emerged behind him. "I don't care if you claim to represent the police. I know my rights! This is harassment and trespassing... And we have witnesses!"

The deliveryman recording on his phone wholeheartedly accepted the indirect invitation to get closer to the action, while the woman with the Dachshund took furtive strides over to the nearest streetlamp.

"Listen up, Stu," Keith began in a measured tone, hooking his thumbs into his belt loops, "Here's how this is gonna go..."

"That's Doctor Sinclair, to you public servants!" Stuart turned an angry shade of red, his mop of silver hair flapping up and down like a second outraged mouth. "And the only thing going anywhere is the two of you – off my property!"

"He's just here for his son," Nolan saw the situation escalating beyond control, and he did his best to undo the noose that Keith had been tying. "Come on, Jesse. We're going on a road trip."

"Tell them, Jesse," Karen stood tall behind Stuart, "Tell your sorry excuse for a father who you'd rather be with."

Riley had Jesse on social media, but he rarely posted anything on his profile.

He looked like he had hit his growth spurt somewhere over the past few years, with a ropey frame and tousled brown hair.

Jesse didn't say a word to either of his parents.

He simply stood glued to the ground, his gaze flitting between the four adults.

He clearly didn't want to be caught up in the middle of their argument.

"Let's go, Jesse," Keith reached past Stuart to grab his son's hand, but Jesse jerked away from him.

"That is assault!" Stuart hollered, reaching into his pocket for his phone. "And attempted kidnapping on top of everything else! I'm calling my lawyer. You're gonna lose your job over this. Both of you!"

"Go ahead, make the call!" Keith dared him, knowing that it wouldn't make any difference after the asteroid hit. "Jesse, get in the damn truck."

"This is ridiculous," Riley exhaled in exasperation from the backseat of the suburban, stealthily tossing her apple core onto Stuart's lawn underneath Keith's pickup.

"I agree," Susan finally leaned her head out through the passenger window. "Karen, I know you're not gonna listen to either of those two, but I hope you'll listen to me. There's an asteroid heading for the West Coast. I don't know when, but the governor and his family have already fled the state. You can do the same, or you can argue yourselves into a crater. Nolan, we're leaving."

For a moment, nobody spoke.

Nobody even moved.

The deliveryman was the first to come back to his senses, cutting off the video to make a phone call as he ran back to his van.

The woman with the Dachshund broke into a jog before the small dog yelped at the end of its leash, gratefully leaping into her arms as she stooped down to scoop it up.

The elderly neighbor's forgotten hose streamed water down the driveway across the street as he ambled into his garage, dropping his car keys on the ground in his haste.

Nolan Armstrong finally found his feet, muttering something to Keith before marching back to the driver's side of the suburban.

"That was a bad move," his lips were dry as he buckled up his seatbelt.

CHAPTER 7

"They're still behind us," Riley gazed over the stacks of supplies and suitcases shuddering against the back window of their red suburban.

Like the handful of his neighbors who had overheard about the asteroid, Stuart Sinclair didn't even think twice about running for his life, grabbing Karen and jumping into his stately white coupe, tailing the Armstrong Family out of the wealthy locale before the rest of Palmview Beach erupted into self-entitled chaos.

Almost as an afterthought, Karen had shrieked at Jesse to jump into Keith's black pickup, since Stuart's coupe was only a two-seater.

Nolan glanced up at the rearview mirror, shaking his head before hanging a right, following Keith's black pickup, the three vehicles charging through the backstreets of the affluent suburb.

"I remember Karen said that Stuart was a doctor," Susan sat up in the front seat to gaze through the back window, "We might need somebody with medical knowledge while we're on the road. There's no telling what we'll run into between here and Nebraska."

"Yeah, it would've been nice to talk about it first though," Nolan replied, clenching his jaw just as tightly as he was clenching the steering wheel, struggling to keep up with Keith's truck as his partner swerved onto the main road and weaved through traffic.

"Hey, at least we're moving now," Riley chimed in from the backseat, belatedly buckling up her own seatbelt as she swayed from side to side with each lurching overtake.

"Besides," Nolan stomped on the accelerator pad to get through an orange light, "Knowing Keith, he might kill Stuart before he even gets the chance to use any of his medical knowledge."

Riley glanced back over her shoulder to see Sinclair speed through the red light, determined to follow them wherever they were going.

Nolan's phone buzzed in the dashboard's cradle, and he was tempted to ignore it, just like he had been ignoring the chatter on his police radio, until "Keith Bowman" flashed across the screen. He slowed down to accept the call.

"Hey, he still on our ass?" Keith's voice growled through the loudspeaker.

"Yeah, he's not letting up," Nolan replied, glancing up at the rearview mirror again. "He just ran that red back there."

"Damn, what I wouldn't give to impound his car right now," Keith joked with a hint of longing in his voice.

"Dad, he's got Mom in the car with him," Jesse Bowman piped up in the background.

"Alright, I'm slowing down," Keith let out a pained sigh before changing the subject. "Nolan, there's a supermarket on the next block. You got everything you need, or do we have to make a stop?"

"We don't have any water," Nolan leaned over the steering wheel to peer at the contents of the black pickup's cargo bed, "Unless you've got a slab in the back?"

"Shit, me too. Let's –"

"Keith," Susan drew closer to the phone in the cradle. "You need to stop *stuttering* while you're on loudspeaker."

"Sorry, Susan," the macho swagger slipped out of his voice. "I'll see you guys in a minute."

As the call ended, Riley couldn't help but admire her mother's ability to cut through the noise of a conversation. It was as if she always waiting to pounce with just the right words to move them along.

The three vehicles pulled into the supermarket's parking lot, impatiently giving way to pedestrians pushing shopping carts laden with groceries.

Riley's family climbed out of the suburban into the sweltering early afternoon heat of Southern California, and she wondered which customers were stocking up their pantries for the week ahead, and which of them were stopping for one last shop before making a break for the next state.

Do any of them know at all? Riley thought to herself.

Everybody looked so calm and collected that it was impossible to tell.

Just as the thought passed through her mind, the sound of screeching tires and rending metal at the parking lot's entrance was enough to make her reconsider.

Everyone craned their necks to get a better view over the rows of parked cars, expecting to see at least one of the drivers storming out of their vehicle to inspect the damage, but neither one of them seemed to think that it was worth their time, not even stopping to argue, or even at the very least, exchange insurance details.

"Looks like a few people have already figured it out," Nolan appeared beside her, rubbing his stubbled jaw.

"You call that driving, Keith!?" Karen's shrill voice pealed across the parking lot as she slammed the white coupe's passenger door, making up for the lack of a road rage-fueled confrontation following the collision at the entrance.

"Susan," Nolan called his wife over, his stern tone returning. "You invited her, she's your problem to deal with. Keith, I need you to watch the supplies, we're not staying long. Riley, with me."

"Yes sir, officer captain, sir," Riley mocked him as soon as they were out of earshot of the others, with Keith more than happy to stay behind to continue arguing with his ex-wife.

"That's my police voice," Nolan smiled for the first time that day as they approached the supermarket's sliding glass doors.

It was a comforting sight.

After all of the chaos and confusion from the moment Riley had seen him striding across their front yard still wearing his police uniform, just seeing her father's smile again – however short-lived – was enough to keep her grounded.

In that moment, she felt like everything was going to be alright.

"Dad, wait," she slipped her phone out of her pocket before they reached the glass entrance, flipping the front camera on them.

"Riley, the whole country's about to fall apart," Nolan chuckled before stopping to put his arm around his daughter, the pair of them grinning for the picture.

"Doesn't mean that we have to," she continued smiling as

she checked the photo.

Her eyebrows furrowed, double tapping the screen to zoom in on a blob of blue and silver prowling through the parking lot behind them.

"Hey, Mr Armstrong!" Stuart Sinclair's voice called as he waited for a car to pass by. He crossed the road with a big fake smile, putting on his best impression of a decent human being. "I think we got off on the wrong foot."

"Come on, let's head inside," Nolan muttered in Riley's ear, his grin already gone.

The supermarket's air-conditioning offered a cool reprieve from the heat shimmering in waves off the parking lot's concrete. Customers shuffled in slow-moving queues as cashiers endured the never-ending bleeps of their cash registers. A bored-looking monotone manager was paging the owner of a station wagon to let them know that they were parked in a loading zone.

Riley breathed a sigh of relief.

After the chaos outside, she was glad to be back in a familiar environment again.

In fact, the only thing spoiling the blissfully ordinary atmosphere was the suddenly sycophantic Stuart Sinclair stalking their steps over to the shopping carts.

"I'm sure we can help each other out," he persisted behind them. "I'd be happy to pay for your groceries!"

"What makes you think we can't afford to buy them ourselves?" Riley whirled around, narrowing her eyes at him.

"I – I wasn't implying, I just..." Sinclair stuttered and stumbled, "A kindness, you see?"

"Grab a cart," Nolan scooted one over to Riley before getting one for himself. He turned back to Stuart, "You're gonna need your own supplies."

"Of course!" Sinclair chirped cheerily, really laying it on thick, "Anything I can do to lighten the load for our group."

They abided the man's presence as they wheeled the three carts down the drinks aisle, past the shelves stacked with soda and energy cans, making a beeline for the jumbo packs of bottled water.

Other customers shot them curious glances as the trio arranged their shopping carts in a semicircle around the shelving bay, loading up as much as their carts could carry.

As if drawn in by an invisible magnet, the onlookers drifted over to the remaining bottles on the shelf, filling up their own carts without even knowing why.

"See if you can find some packets of peanuts," Nolan suggested as they left the growing crowd clanging their carts together in the drinks aisle, "I'll grab a couple boxes of protein bars and some toilet paper."

"Don't we have enough food already?" Riley asked, hesitant to split up.

"For now," he nodded, glancing over his shoulder at the other shoppers as they called for a store attendant to check whether there was any more bottled water in the back. "But this might be the last time we come across a stocked supermarket for a while."

"Come on, I know this store," Stuart interrupted as he pulled up beside them, his fake smile fading with the physical strain of pushing his laden cart. "Nuts are this way. The health foods are just one aisle over."

Riley's feeling of uncertainty dissipated as she and her father turned in the same direction after Sinclair, only separated by a single column of shelves.

She brushed stray strands of hair over her ear as she bent down to pull hanging packets of peanuts and almonds and cashews off the rack.

"Excuse me, dear," someone tapped her on the shoulder from behind. She turned to see an elderly woman smiling back at her. "Is there a sale on?"

Riley glanced sidelong at the stacks of bottled water in her cart, unsure of what to say. Sinclair was at the other end of the aisle, slotting boxes of crackers wherever they would fit into his own cart.

"Yes," she lied, hoping that it would be the end of the conversation.

"That's handy," the elderly woman cooed, drawing her cart alongside Riley's. "Sometimes, I prefer to drink bottled water. You never know what they put in the taps these days! Say, would you mind if I pinched one of yours? Even if I found where they put the stupid things, my old bones won't be able to lift one by myself."

"Sure," Riley dropped the last packets of nuts in with her haul, before hoisting a slab of bottled water into the elderly woman's cart.

She figured that it was a small price to pay to send the old woman on her way.

She had more than enough to spare anyway.

"Hey, do you work here?" a man called from the end of the aisle, followed by two sweaty boys in soiled baseball uniforms. He strode towards her without waiting for an answer, "This place is a madhouse. Even the sports drinks are gone."

"I'm a customer," Riley attempted to pull her shopping cart out of reach, having done her good deed for the day, but her haul was too heavy for her to move in a hurry.

"Are you gonna drink all that by yourself?" the man asked sarcastically, grabbing a slab of water out of her cart before she could protest. Holding his prize in the crook of his elbow, he retreated a step to gauge her reaction, and then he reached in for another. "That's for being selfish. Look boys, see what happens to selfish people." He grinned back at her, seizing the opportunity to deliver a life lesson to his two sons, "Hey, everyone! There's water over here!"

He shook his head in disgust as Riley wrenched at the handlebar, throwing her weight backwards in the direction of the cash registers.

She was mid-turn when a handful of shoppers rounded the corner.

Sinclair was already gone.

Riley's breath hitched in her throat as they advanced on her.

She felt like she was drowning, and she started sucking in lungfuls of air to compensate, unaware that her chest was already heaving. Black stars swam in the corners of her eyes, and she leaned over the shopping cart just to hold herself upright.

"Dad!" she managed to call out between ragged breaths.

"I'm here," Nolan Armstrong appeared at the other end of the aisle, crashing his cart into the shelves as the man and his two baseballer sons slunk past. "Everybody stand aside!"

The mob balked as he held his police badge aloft, like predatory animals transfixed by the dancing flames of a firebrand. With his free hand, Nolan completed Riley's turning circle, steering her cart back towards the cash registers.

"You can have whatever's in my cart," he offered them in a steady tone, nodding at Riley to start pushing. "Just let us pass, and it's all yours."

Riley staggered forward against the cart's handlebar, still fighting to get her breathing back under control.

"I just got off the phone with my brother, y'all," a big blurry woman was the first to break the spell, "He said there's an asteroid gon' hit the city. One cart ain't gon' be enough if the water gets shut off!"

"I say we take it all!"

"One pig can't arrest all of us!"

"Let's see how he likes his own handcuffs!"

The next thing Riley knew, Nolan was hauling her by the arm back up the aisle, stopping momentarily to throw his own shopping cart onto its side, water bottles bursting out through the plastic wrap packaging and rolling across the floor.

Riley kept her mouth closed and held one nostril shut as they searched for an empty aisle, double backing towards the cash registers, where a pair of businessmen were tugging at opposite ends of the elderly woman's single slab of water.

Nolan shoved his way through the teeming mass of panic buyers flooding the cashiers, leading Riley through the sliding glass doors back out into the sweltering early afternoon heat.

Riley doubled over to take deep breaths of fresh air, while her father rubbed the heel of his hand between her shoulder blades.

"Sinclair!!" he roared across the parking lot as he caught sight of the silver-haired doctor. "Riley, we need to move."

"I'm okay," she nodded, standing up straight again, letting him lead her across the road all the same.

Stuart pretended that he hadn't heard his name being called, preoccupied with hastily loading up the back of his white coupe. He slammed the trunk shut just as Riley and Nolan caught up to him.

"Where the hell were you?" Nolan grabbed Sinclair by his

blue tracksuit's collar, backing him up against his own car.

"You left me, you asshole," Riley's voice dripped with contempt.

"I'm sorry," Stuart squirmed with a completely unapologetic tone, feebly flailing out of Nolan's grip and straightening up his jacket with a huff. "I was focused on the objective. What happened to your water? Oh, that's right. You were too busy giving it all away to everyone else."

"You son of a bitch, my daugh–"

"Correction," Stuart waggled one of his thick sausage fingers in the air, "*Doctor Sinclair*, who also happens to have all of the water. And if you want to share any of the water that *I* just paid for, you'll have to bring me along."

CHAPTER 8

"Where's the water?" Keith Bowman jumped down from the cargo bed of his black pickup, staring at Riley and Nolan's empty hands with a puzzled expression.

"Sinclair's got it," Nolan confessed with a pained sigh. He glanced over at the two women standing beside Jesse's window at the front of the truck. "Susan, Karen, come on. Let's saddle up."

"Don't tell me he's coming with us," Keith frowned, his stony gaze switching between Riley and Nolan.

"Only a matter of time before we crash if we try shaking them again," Nolan rubbed his stubbled jaw, studying his partner's face before adding, "I've already given him the address."

"Fuck, Nolan!" Keith glared at the smiling silver-haired doctor across the parking lot, Stuart holding his white coupe's passenger door open for Karen. "Old Limp Dick's gonna get us all killed before we even see the asteroid."

"Well, if he falls behind, he's on his own," Riley narrowed her eyes at the self-serving son of a bitch, already eager to return the favor of letting him fend for himself.

Keith grunted in wholehearted agreement.

Screeching tires sounded from the street beyond the parking lot as a sports car swerved into the oncoming traffic lanes just before an intersection, securing pole position at the lights.

"We better get back on the road before it gets any worse," Nolan pulled his keys from his pocket.

"Keep the channel open until we're outta the city," Keith hustled around the side of his black crew cab pickup. "I'll take point."

The Armstrongs climbed back into the red suburban, Susan staring out the window with her arms folded in the front passenger seat.

"Could you tell your partner to watch his mouth around our daughter?" she eyed Keith's truck bitterly as the vulgar man kicked it into reverse, extra irritable after her placating exchange with Karen.

"Susan, you've been telling him for years," Nolan locked eyes with Riley in the backseat as he looked over his shoulder to back the car out, harboring the faintest hint of a smile. "What difference will it make if I say it?"

"It'll make a difference *to me*," Susan stared sidelong at him as they followed Keith's pickup out of the parking lot.

"It's not a big deal, Mom," Riley came to her father's rescue as he shifted uncomfortably in the driver's seat. "I'm not a kid anymore, I can handle it."

The phone in the dashboard's cradle buzzed, with "Keith Bowman" flashing across the screen.

Nolan let out an ill-timed chuckle that he attempted to disguise as a cough, wilting under his wife's icy glare.

"Look, I'll tell him when we get to Nebraska," his thumb hovered over the phone as they turned onto the road. "We've got a long ways to go, and I need him focused. We might miss something crucial if he gets distracted by having to run his words through a filter."

"Everybody got their tickets ready for the shit show!?" Keith yelled through the loudspeaker as they took off down the street.

So crucial, Susan mouthed at her husband, shaking her head.

Keeping his eyes on the road, Nolan turned down the volume of the chatter coming through his police radio so that it wouldn't interfere with the call.

Riley gazed outside the window as they drove through the stop-start traffic of the commercial district, watching panic ripple through the streets of Redhurst.

It was as if the act of answering a phone call or merely glancing down at the screen in their hand was transforming people into irrational lunatics. And as an increasing number of strolling pedestrians were spontaneously sprinting down the sidewalks, more and more people began checking their phones to find out what was happening.

A man with a barber's cape still draped around his shoulders ran in front of the Armstrong Family's red suburban, his head half-shaven. Nolan blared the horn, and the man held up his hands in confused terror, his wild eyes searching for the next break in traffic before lunging into the next lane. He was almost clipped by a convertible before reaching his parked car on the other side of the street.

Wary of anyone else desperate enough to risk running into traffic, Riley wound up her window as they stopped behind Keith's truck at a set of red lights.

A construction worker rounded the corner of the intersection, holding her yellow hardhat steady with one hand while carrying a road sign with the other. Sizing up her options, she found a likely target, and took two steps into the street to poleaxe a courier off his bicycle.

Nolan slammed his hand down on the central door lock as three more road workers came charging around the corner.

"Keith! Run this red!!" he yelled at the phone in the cradle, one hand reaching for his holstered pistol as they watched one of the construction workers pull a middle-aged woman out through the open window of her luxury sedan.

"Two seconds!" Keith shouted back, and an instant later, a fuel truck barreled across the intersection. The black pickup's tires screeched as he peeled off, with their red suburban and Sinclair's white coupe following closely behind. Spurred on by their momentum, the fourth car to run the set of traffic lights wasn't so lucky, getting cleaned up by a tour bus. Keith's voice came back dry through the loudspeaker, "I could write you up for incitement, Officer Armstrong."

"Put it on my tab," Nolan breathed, glancing up at the crushed hatchback in the rearview mirror as they approached the traffic banked up at the next intersection. "There's gonna be a whole lot more of that if we wanna make it outta the city alive."

"I wouldn't be so sure," Keith replied, his arm reaching out of the pickup's window to affix a blue cylinder to the top of his truck. "Nobody's heading back to the coast. We got two lanes free."

Blue LED strobes flashed from the police beacon as Keith veered across the double dividing lines. Out of habit, Nolan instinctively glanced over his shoulder to check for any approaching vehicles before pulling out after his partner, with Sinclair and a few other opportunistic drivers tacking themselves onto the back of the makeshift police convoy.

With the occasional westbound vehicle pulling over to get out of the way, they made good time through the bulk of the city's traffic, only having to slow down to nose their way through intersections and the grisly scenes of vehicular collisions.

Dazed drivers and bleeding passengers staggered out from behind smoking wrecks, relieved to see the flashing blue lights approaching, only to watch as the emergency beacon cruised past before disappearing into the distance again.

Riley stared in stunned silence as they ventured through the heart of the city, the unfolding scenes of desperation only getting worse.

Caught behind bumper-to-bumper traffic along a busy boulevard, one bus driver took his chances with mounting the curb. For a while, the gambit paid off, and it was smooth sailing for the half dozen passengers on board, even keeping time with the makeshift police convoy on the other side of the road.

That was, until the sidewalk began to taper in, becoming too narrow to navigate. With the next intersection in the near distance, the driver decided to plow on ahead. The panicked passengers flung themselves from the emergency window as the bus carved a path of destruction along the sidewalk, leaving a trail of smashed signboards, torn awnings and mangled displays in its wake.

Riley had to look away as the improvised bus route came to an abrupt end, the driver slumping over the steering wheel with the coppery taste of regret in his mouth, sandwiched between his seat and a telephone pole.

Farther on up the road, Keith's truck slowed to weave through a massive pile-up at an intersection on the corner of a small strip mall. Security alarms pealed above the noise of blaring car horns as a gang of looters raided a liquor store's shelves.

Riley managed to spot one sane person – by comparison, at

least – among the crazed lunatics plaguing the intersection. Sitting alone in a bus shelter on the other side of the road was a bloodied businessman, his tie loosened and shirt sleeves rolled up, taking resigned swigs from a bottle of bourbon as he waited for a bus that would never come.

"JESSE, GET DOWN!!" Keith yelled through the loudspeaker as *cracks* of gunfire sounded from the strip mall.

Riley jerked forward as a group of thugs flashed metal outside a pawn shop, but her seatbelt locked up and threw her back against the seat.

Unable to think straight with bullets flying through the air, she grabbed the seatbelt's strap over her shoulder and yanked hard, twice, before thumbing the release and throwing her knees to the floor mat, ducking her head in between the two front seats.

Peering above her mother's head buried in the center console, she could see the pawn shop owner returning fire, one of the looters doubling over in the parking lot.

Their would-be getaway driver must have caught a glimpse of Keith's police beacon, because the idling brown station wagon parked nearby burned rubber as it tore out of the strip mall's lot, abandoning the rest of the looters to find their own way out of the city – if they survived the fight.

Nolan had one white-knuckled hand on the steering wheel as he leaned over Susan, shielding her. He had his head raised just enough to see the roof of Keith's black pickup over the dashboard, hesitating to hit the accelerator pad as the truck sped up and out of sight.

"Talk to me, Keith, where'd you go!?" he shouted at the phone in the cradle.

"Go straight, road's clear!" Keith yelled back over the gunfire,

"I've got you in my rearview. You're good – stomp that shit!!"

Without being able to see the road ahead, Nolan gunned the engine, having complete faith in his partner, even with his family's lives on the line. They drove blind until the barking bullets faded in the distance, and he swung himself back up behind the steering wheel.

"Everybody good!?" he asked as Riley and Susan slowly sat upright in their seats, his gaze switching sidelong and up at the rearview mirror and back again.

"I'm alright," Riley breathed hard as she reached over her shoulder for her seatbelt, the strap locking up again as if it was deliberately trying to torment her.

"Fucking crazy day, huh?" Keith chuckled through the loudspeaker.

"Fucking crazy day," Susan echoed, breaking her own rule.

"Mom, watch your mouth," Riley scolded her with a smirk from the backseat. "What kinda example are you trying to set?"

Susan gasped as she remembered herself, shooting a guilty glance at Nolan, before the three of them burst out laughing, unwinding the nervous tension in the car as their edgy adrenaline ebbed away in waves.

"Did Mom and Stuart make it out?" Jesse's voice piped up over the loudspeaker.

"Oh, who gives a shit?" Keith snorted, still drunk with elation.

"I'll check," Riley glanced over her shoulder at the convoy of cars and vans and trucks wending their way around the pile-up, still following their lead. She caught sight of Sinclair's white coupe emerging and slumped back in her seat. "Yeah, they're still behind us."

"Can't win them all," Keith supposed before slowing down

again, "Looks like we've got a crowd up ahead. We clear them and it's a straight shot to the freeway."

Riley leaned forward in the backseat, furrowing her eyebrows at the sidewalks bustling with pedestrians.

There was no traffic to be seen – other than the line of cars behind Sinclair – and at first glance, it seemed like there was some sort of a street festival.

Looking closer though, she could see people carrying bundles of designer clothes, gaming consoles and plasma TVs.

The press of people grew thicker on the next block, with a teeming mass of looters pulsing in and out of a row of commercial storefronts.

Farther on down the road, vandals were taking turns at throwing trash cans at the reinforced glass panes of a jewelry store, the lone security guard inside cowering with the rest of the sales attendants behind the counter.

"What the fu–" Keith's phone call dropped just as an empty clothing rack sailed out of the crowd to collide with the side of his pickup.

"Pig!" one of the looters yelled above the noise of the mob as another volley of debris hit the truck.

"It's his police beacon," Nolan clenched his jaw as he thumbed his phone in the cradle, "Dial Keith Bowman."

A three-tone *out of service* chime played through the loud-speaker.

"What's his number?" Susan pulled out her phone, only to stare at the upper corner of her screen. She slapped the back of her phone against her palm and anxiously checked it again before turning back to Nolan, "Mine's out too. What do we do?"

"He's a target with that light on his truck," he turned up the volume on his police radio and thumbed the switch, "Keith, turn the light off!"

"Multiple collisions downtown, can I get an ambu–"

"Shots fired in Palmview, need back–"

"Dispatch!? Where the hell are –"

Nolan clenched his jaw as he muted the radio again. Glancing around at the crowd, he blasted the horn instead, as if honking would relay his message. It only served to bring more attention to the blue LED strobe flashing on the roof of Keith's pickup.

Riley hunched over in her seat, cupping her hands over her peripheral vision as the mob of looters pressed in on them from both sides.

It felt as though the sidewalks were squeezing the street like the clamps of a colossal vise, and on a deeper, more sinister level, she could feel an invisible set of pincers reaching into the suburban to crush her chest.

All she could do was focus on her breathing.

Just as the first few pairs of hands smacked against their windows, a deafening explosion sounded from somewhere up ahead, followed by two smaller blasts, *crack – crack*, much closer.

Riley looked up to see Nolan holding his handgun out the window, pointing it up at the sky. A shotgun barrel was smoking out of Keith's window.

The crowd backed away from the warning shots as Keith's truck revved its engine menacingly, his shotgun barrel slowly tilting down towards a trio of teenage looters still standing in front of the pickup.

"Don't do it, don't do it," Nolan murmured underneath his breath, even as the mob began to find its courage again, calling the makeshift police convoy on their bluff.

A trash can arced through the air, landing in the pickup

truck's cargo bed, and Keith gunned the engine.

Two of the vandals dived out of the way just in time, but the truck knocked over a third.

Riley's stomach threatened to fly up into her throat as the red suburban bounced over the teenager's body.

Looking back over her shoulder, she watched as the long convoy of cars and vans and trucks left red streaks in the street, some of the vehicles even swerving intentionally to add to the body count.

She fought the taste of her own bile.

CHAPTER 9

Parking garages, office buildings and apartment complexes stood tall on either side of the empty street as the freeway loomed overhead in the distance. A cacophony of car horns trumpeted from the foot of the on-ramp, the discordant orchestra traveling the entire length of the tumultuous traffic crawling across the overpass.

"Where's he going?" Riley perked up in the backseat as Keith Bowman took an unexpected turn, pulling his black pickup into a multi-level parking garage half a block away from the freeway's entrance.

"I don't know," Nolan spun the steering wheel, "But we're not splitting up."

Riley looked out through the back window of their red suburban as the rest of the impromptu convoy faltered, unsure of whether to follow the flashing emergency lights into the parking garage or try their luck with getting onto the freeway.

Quickly making up his mind, Stuart Sinclair took the turn after them, the low undercarriage of his stately white coupe scraping the steeply sloped entrance with a satisfyingly harsh grate.

An orange vintage muscle car began signaling for the garage as well, and was mid-turn when a food delivery truck surged past.

The muscle car's wheels straightened up before roaring underneath the freeway after the truck, the rest of the vehicles in the convoy soon breaking off to follow suit, subconsciously selecting the driver of the delivery truck as their next best shepherd to safety.

The engines of the black pickup, the red suburban and the white coupe rumbled as they spiraled up the corkscrew ramp along the side of the multi-level structure, the noise magnified by the vast empty spaces in the near-deserted parking garage.

Riley and her parents shielded their eyes as the late afternoon sun winked through the windshield with every turn, the glaring Southern Californian sunset impossible to ignore.

Besides their three vehicles, there were no signs of life across the barren concrete expanse on top of the parking garage. Even if the West Coast wasn't being threatened by the advent of the apocalypse, Riley couldn't imagine the parking lot appearing anything other than abandoned underneath the unforgiving Californian sun.

Keith shut off his engine alongside the waist-high wall lining the edge of the parking lot, his black crew cab pickup easily spanning the length of three car spaces. Jesse Bowman jumped out of the passenger side, skirting around the front to inspect the truck's grille.

Nolan Armstrong rubbed his stubbled jaw before pulling up behind his partner.

"What's the hold up!?" Stuart's mop of silver hair flopped out the window of his white coupe, blaring the horn before even giving them enough time to formulate a response.

"Can you tell your guests to give us a minute?" Nolan gave his wife a sidelong glance as they climbed out of the red suburban.

"I wasn't the one who invited them to Nebraska," Susan reminded him, shutting the passenger door on his stunned realization that he was equally as responsible for Stuart and Karen's insufferable presence.

It was an easy choice for Riley to decide which one of her parents she wanted to follow. She kept a respectful distance behind her father as he approached his partner's truck, trying her best not to appear too nosy.

"Dumbass fucking kid," Keith popped the lever for the engine's hood before tilting his seat back to stare up at the pickup's ceiling upholstery. "What the fuck was he thinking, just standing there?"

"It wasn't your fault," Nolan glanced back at Riley with his eyebrows raised, a subtle cue for her to keep on walking, "You did what you had to do. And we're alive because of it."

"Don't hit me with that same fucking line!" Keith choked, raising a hand to his face, his eyes hidden from view behind the truck cab's center pillar. "It's happening all over again."

Riley picked up her pace, passing by Jesse as he leaned over the engine.

He glanced up at her with a grim expression.

They used to be close.

Of course they had been close — they had been the only two kids sitting at the table every time their families went out for dinner.

They had practically grown up together.

He had changed so much ever since his parents had gotten a divorce.

Wanting to avoid any awkward attempts at trying to reconnect after years of not seeing each other, Riley whipped out her phone and kept on moving, pretending that she had notifications to check.

Just like those of her parents, Riley's phone was out of service as well. Toggling her connection settings did nothing to help. She had thought that the height of the parking garage would have made a difference in the dead zone, but apparently not.

Riley wondered how many of her friends were on their way out of Redhurst right now, but there was no way for her to know for certain without a signal.

Calvin had said that he would message her later.

Maybe his blue sedan had been part of the long line of vehicles traveling in their convoy.

With the sun at her back, Riley slid her phone back into her jeans pocket and gazed out over the edge of the parking garage.

Headlights and taillights dotted the freeway below, cars and vans and trucks stretching for miles in either direction, every lane of traffic moving so slowly that they appeared almost stationary.

There was no way that they would be able to leave the state via the freeway.

At the snail's pace of the traffic flow, Riley doubted that they would even be clear of Redhurst's outer city limits by the morning.

Through the windows of an apartment building across the street, she could see a pair of kids setting the dining table for dinner. In a living room on another floor, a woman dressed in tight gym clothes was stretching before going through the motions of her exercise routine. In an adjacent apartment, a boy in his mid-teens was poking around behind his computer desk, his game frozen with an error on the screen.

It seemed that not everyone had bought into the panic of the approaching asteroid. After all, as far as Riley knew, everyone was relying purely on rumors spread by word of mouth. Even her own father had no concrete evidence that the asteroid was going to hit the West Coast, other than the governor's request for a police escort to the airport.

What if this is all just a big coincidence, she wondered to herself.

Maybe the governor had just picked the wrong day to go on a family vacation, and everything had been blown way out of proportion.

No, it had to be real.

Too much had already happened for it all to be a case of mass hysteria.

People were dead in the streets.

There was no coming back from that.

A tear trickled down her cheek as reality settled in, and she rubbed it away angrily before glancing back at the trio of idling vehicles.

The asteroid was real, and it was coming whether they liked it or not.

They had to keep moving.

"Are you two done with your little mother's group meeting?" Stuart Sinclair huffed as he shuffled towards Keith's black pickup. "We just lost our place in the lead because of this pointless detour."

"Back off, Sinclair," Nolan turned around with his hands on his hips. "How about you go grab us some water?"

"You've got some nerve," Stuart waggled one of his thick sausage fingers in the air. "How about you get back in your damn vehicle and get us the hell outta the city? Then *maybe* I'll let you have some of *my* water!"

Having heard enough, Keith climbed out of his truck, slamming the door.

"There's the freeway, asshole," he grabbed the back of Sinclair's chubby neck and turned his head in case he had missed it. "Get yourself out."

"We can't take the freeway," Riley called back from the edge of the parking garage. "The traffic's barely moving."

"They'll move for that police light though," Sinclair wrenched himself out of Keith's grasp, fixing the collar of his blue tracksuit before jerking his gaze up at the beacon on top of the pickup's roof.

"Not everybody," Nolan countered somberly with a sideways glance at his partner.

"Then we *make* them move," Stuart's eyes shifted between the two men before settling on Keith. "We all saw you run that lowlife looter down. You've got what it takes to clear a path forward. Doing what needs to be done. To hell with the rest of them!"

"You have no idea," Keith averted his gaze, turning to release his truck's hood prop and gesturing for Jesse to back up.

"That's the spirit," Sinclair beamed broadly at them all, happy to get back on the road. "So, let's turn arou—"

"YOU HAVE NO FUCKING IDEA!!" Keith slammed the hood down, making Jesse retreat around the side of the pickup. Nolan held Keith back as he advanced on Stuart, "Taking someone's life, like it's that easy! That kid froze. He didn't wanna be there. He didn't wanna fucking die!"

"Don't tell me you're having another breakdown, Keith!" Karen's shrill voice echoed across the concrete expanse, Susan throwing her arms up in frustration beside the white coupe. "Get over yourself, already!"

51

"Perhaps I've misjudged you," Sinclair shrugged, feigning disappointment. Standing safely out of harm's way behind Nolan, Stuart decided to goad Keith even further, "Perhaps you don't have what it takes after all... No wonder your family left you."

Nolan stared sidelong at the unbridled fury contorting his partner's face.

Something unspoken passed between the two men.

Nolan swallowed, and nodded.

Dropping his arms, he sidestepped out of the way, letting Keith unleash his rage.

Horror-struck, Stuart turned and fled, making it as far as the pickup's rear wheel before Keith tackled him to the ground, straddling the man's backside and raining savage blows into his fleshy shoulder blades.

Sinclair's yelps of pain mingled with Karen's shrieks and wails across the parking lot.

All Riley could see were Keith's elbows cocking back before delivering another fist, while Stuart's meaty arms flailed along the ground, his fat sausage fingers scrabbling around the concrete, searching desperately for something to throw Keith off his back.

"Dad, this is crazy!" as much as Riley hated Sinclair, this was getting out of hand.

"It's been a long time coming," Nolan hugged her, blocking her view as he stared intently at the freeway. "The sooner they settle this, the sooner we'll be back on the –"

CRACK!!

The sound of a gunshot bullwhipped across the sunbaked concrete of the parking lot.

"Keith," Nolan's arms fell from around Riley as he hesitantly looked over his shoulder. "What did you do?"

Riley staggered backwards a step.

Keith Bowman was holding his hands up, shaking his head. The holster of his police kit belt was smoking.

Sinclair was still on the ground, lying down on his side, with his thick fingers wrapped around Keith's pistol.

"Get off me," Stuart snarled, pointing the barrel squarely at Keith's chest.

"Easy now," Keith slowly rose to his feet, backing up towards Riley and Nolan.

"Don't talk to me about *easy!*" Sinclair wheezed as he scrambled upright, keeping the gun on the two men. "*Easy* was getting back in your vehicle and getting us outta the city. *You* took the hard way. *You're* the one responsible for bringing us all up here."

"Stuart!" Karen's shrill voice pealed across the parking lot. "What are you doing!?"

"I'm doing what needs to be done!" with an agonized twist in his mouth, Sinclair reached up to grab the blue police beacon from the black pickup's roof, breaking the magnet's bond and ripping the cord's plug out of the cigarette lighter. "*Somebody* has to around here."

"Stuart, calm down," Jesse's voice broke in from the other side of the truck. "Please, just lower the gun."

"And where were you when your father was on top of me?" Sinclair shot an accusing glare at Jesse before retraining the gun on Nolan and Keith. "After all the kindness I showed you for the sake of your mother, it's abundantly clear to me who you favor... I'm glad I brought the coupe."

Riley gazed sidelong at her father, waiting for him to do something, *anything*, when her pupils dilated, her eyes dropping to the glistening red stain spreading on the side of his uniform, halfway up his torso.

"Dad?" her voice sounded small and distant and unnatural in her own ears, as if somebody else had said it. Her chest began heaving with shallow breaths as her eyes filled with the sight of his blood.

"Don't you move!" Sinclair threatened as Nolan turned towards Riley.

"Nolan!?" Susan cried, running towards him as he dropped to one knee, his mouth hanging open, eyes wide with confusion.

"No – no, no, no," Keith turned to see his partner collapse onto his hands and knees. "Jesse, get my first aid kit under the seat!"

"Which seat!?" Jesse pulled the passenger side door open, jumping into the pickup and searching the back.

Riley felt like a prisoner trapped in her own body, unable to move, unable to think, unable to do anything but watch as her father fell face forward, bleeding on the ground.

"Officer down!" Keith yelled into his police radio, cranking the volume up.

"Dispatch isn't responding," a lone woman's voice crackled back. "I've gotta get back to my husband. Sorry, brother. We're on our own."

"FUCK!!" Keith paced back and forth before looking back at his truck. "Jesse! Come on!!"

"He – he shouldn't have been standing there," Stuart stammered, the gun in his hand rattling as he realized what he had done. He dragged the police beacon's cord along the concrete as he stumbled back towards his coupe. "This – this is all your fault, Keith! We shouldn't have been up here!"

Keith ignored Sinclair as he ripped the buttons of his own

police uniform open, tearing it from his sweaty undershirt and bundling up the cloth before kneeling down beside Nolan, leaning his weight into his partner's glistening torso.

"We need to wash the wound!" Karen was bent over the coupe's open trunk, lifting a slab of water bottles from the back.

"Dad?" Riley fell to her knees, hands trembling over his face as his lips began to turn blue. She had no idea what to do.

"Get back in the car," Sinclair ordered his wife, still holding the gun up as he slammed the trunk shut with his elbow. "Or stay here with them."

"But we can't just leave them!" Karen was halfway towards the pickup truck when Stuart climbed back into the coupe.

She shot her son a glance of dismay, weighing up her options, before dropping the slab of water to the ground and running back towards the coupe.

"You fucking bitch!" Susan's fingers scrabbled at Nolan's holster in anger.

"Give me that," Keith unbuttoned the strap, withdrew the pistol and flipped the safety off in one fluid movement, "Keep pressure on the wound."

Still on one knee, Keith lined up the gun's sights on Sinclair's coupe as the tires screeched towards the exit ramp.

He squeezed the trigger three times, one shot shattering the taillight, the next one punching a hole in the trunk, and the third puncturing the rear wheel.

Stuart overcompensated for the sudden loss of traction, scraping the side of his coupe against the concrete wall as they turned down the spiraling ramp.

It wasn't enough to stop them though, and they soon disappeared out of sight.

"Dad, say something, please!" tears streamed down Riley's cheeks as she choked on her own sobs.

CHAPTER 10

"He's going into shock," Keith Bowman grunted as he laid Nolan's pistol on the ground.

"Here, Dad," Jesse dropped the first aid kit beside the front of the pickup truck.

"Go get me that water," Keith unzipped the bag and ripped out a pair of scissors.

Jesse took off running towards the slab of water bottles across the parking lot as Keith began cutting a hole through Nolan's police uniform.

"Is he gonna be okay?" Riley wiped her eyes, taking deep breaths to control her shuddering. "What can I do?"

"See if you can get a signal," Susan's teeth were clenched as she leaned all of her weight into his torso. "We need an ambulance."

Riley pulled her phone from her pocket, her heart sinking to see that it was still out of service. Fresh tears swam in her eyes as she stared down at her father's cheek pressed to the concrete, dust swirling with each ragged breath.

Susan removed the bloody bundle of Keith's shirt as his scissors cut through the cloth around the wound.

"I can stitch him back up," Keith inspected Nolan's torso, blood weeping from the bullet hole between two ribs. He looked up at Riley and Susan. "But I can't take the bullet out. He'll be okay, but he's gonna need surgery."

Riley nodded with a sigh of relief.

Her father was going to be okay.

That was all she needed to hear.

Not wasting any more time, she turned on her heel and jogged over to the other side of the roof, staring intently at the upper corner of her phone's screen.

Out of service.

Biting her bottom lip, she glanced at the door to the stairwell, wondering if she could use the handrail as an antenna to boost her signal.

She looked back at her mother and Keith huddling over her father as Jesse slid a rolled-up towel underneath his head to serve as a makeshift pillow.

He was in good hands.

Riley threw the stairwell's door open and stepped inside, suppressing a gag as the inner city stench of concentrated urine pervaded her nostrils.

She held the back of her phone against the staircase's metal railing, giving it a few seconds before trying different angles.

Still no luck.

She was about to head back out onto the roof when she realized that she wouldn't need a signal if she could just find a landline.

Remembering the people who had stayed behind in the apartment building across the street, she stowed her phone back into her pocket and ran down the stairs.

The scuffs of her sneakers echoed in the stairwell as she took the steps two at a time, her footfalls drumming in synchronization to the pulse pounding in her ears.

Food scraps and takeaway containers and empty beer bottles littered the corners of the stairwell, along with the occasional musty-smelling stain.

Riley didn't mind it though.

After being cooped up in the backseat, powerless to do anything but watch as the rest of the city fell into anarchy, it felt good to finally be doing something to help.

Breathless, with her head spinning in circles, Riley hit the ground floor, almost crashing into the underside of the last staircase as she turned to keep on running.

She locked out her knees and skidded to a stop, falling backwards onto the floor before scrambling to her feet again.

Panting hard, she threw the door open, the bang against the wall echoing out into the ground floor of the empty parking garage and back up the stairwell.

Taking a moment to get her bearings straight, she staggered alongside the concrete wall towards the garage's entrance, looking across the street as she tried to remember which one was the apartment building she had seen.

She supposed that it wouldn't make much of a difference which building she chose.

They would all have landlines, especially if the people living inside were in the middle of a dead zone.

Standing curbside, Riley was about to run across the street when an ice cream truck flew past. She must have been mere inches from the truck's side mirror, because she could feel the residual wind current whooshing past her face as her hair whipped up in the slipstream.

Taking a step back, she brushed her hair back behind her ears, looking both ways this time.

Her heart skipped a beat as she glanced towards the freeway's overpass, still half a block away. The on-ramp had cleared up now, but just a few car-lengths from its entrance sat Sinclair's white coupe.

Riley crept closer down the sidewalk, hiding behind a light pole.

"I know I've got a spare wheel in here," Stuart grunted as he unloaded slabs of water bottles from the trunk, air hissing from his rear tire. "Do you know how to work a jack?"

"Jesse knows," Karen folded her arms, looking up at the parking garage's roof. "My son is up there, and you just left him."

"So did you," Sinclair reminded her curtly as he massaged a throb in his lower back. "Now make yourself useful and help me change this wheel."

Sorry, Dad, Riley bit her bottom lip as she crouched behind the light pole. *The ambulance is just gonna have to wait.*

She had already seen her father in hospital a few times after he had been shot in the line of duty, and he had always pulled through, making full recoveries from worse injuries.

Admittedly, seeing his blood in the heat of the moment had been unnerving, but the man was near invincible.

A few more minutes wouldn't make much of a difference.

Justice couldn't wait though – not while Sinclair was trying to flee the scene.

Riley swallowed dryly as she waited for the perfect opportunity to strike.

She was going to make the self-centered son of a bitch pay for what he did to her father.

Karen was rotating the jack while Stuart was on his knees

beside the punctured wheel with a ratchet at the ready.

They had their backs turned.

They wouldn't even see Riley coming until she was on top of them.

She stalked out from behind the light pole, ready to break out into a headlong sprint, when she heard a pair of sneakers scuffing the pavement, and a split second later, two unseen arms grabbed her from behind.

CHAPTER 11

Riley wrenched at the veiny pair of masculine arms wrapped around her torso, struggling in muffled silence with her elbows pinned to her sides.

She didn't make a noise, careful not to alert Stuart and Karen farther down the street.

Even if she did scream, she doubted that either of them would come running to her rescue.

She had to deal with this threat by herself.

Relying on the muscle memory of her father's lessons, Riley dropped her weight and spread her feet wide apart, trying to prevent whoever was behind her from lifting her into the air or throwing her off balance. She grabbed his veiny forearms for additional support as he began hauling her backwards towards the entrance of the parking garage.

Despite his viselike grip, she was still capable of escaping.

All she had to do was swish her hips to one side, drop her hand to his groin and *squeeze*.

But she didn't want him to scream and give away her position to Sinclair.

The unseen assailant was already dragging her into the

shadows of the parking garage before Riley began to consider that he might not have been acting alone.

She had only ever trained to handle herself against one attacker.

She had to break free of the bear hug before it was too late.

With Stuart and Karen out of sight, Riley wrapped her hand around one of the man's forefingers and bent it backwards – like it was just a stick of wood waiting to be snapped – instantly making him release his hold as he hissed in pain.

Pivoting on the balls of her feet, she twisted her would-be attacker's wrist so that he spun around, dancing on his tiptoes as she walked him backwards, pulling his finger like a joystick all the while, determined to make his fingernail touch the back of his hand.

"Stop, stop, stop," he gasped as she kicked out the back of his knee, his face twisted in writhing agony as he stared up at her, pleading for mercy. "It's me!"

"What the *hell*, Jesse?" she furrowed her eyebrows at him, keeping a firm grip on his finger until he explained himself.

"They told me to come find you," Jesse Bowman panted on his knees, still wincing in pain even though she had already stopped bending his forefinger beyond its normal range of motion.

"Did they tell you to tackle me, too?" Riley let him go, shoving him over in exasperation.

"I saw what you were about to do," Jesse climbed to his feet and dusted off his knees before turning to face her. "I had to stop you."

"He shot my dad," she scowled at him before moving back towards the garage's entrance, peering out at the street. Sinclair was still struggling to take the punctured wheel off the coupe.

63

Riley glanced back over her shoulder, "I don't care if he's your stepdad. You'd be doing the same thing if he shot Keith."

"It's not about that," Jesse put his hand on her arm before she could step back out onto the sidewalk again.

"Then what?" she glared pointedly at his hand.

"You haven't even thought this through, have you?" Jesse pulled his arm back and decided to keep his distance this time, remembering just how close he had come to a snapped finger. "Stuart still has the gun. And a ratchet. And my mom's with him."

"So?" Riley asked angrily, although even if she didn't want to admit it to Jesse, she had to admit it to herself – she didn't have a plan.

She glanced back at the street.

Sinclair was rolling his spare wheel around the back of the coupe.

In a moment, he would have his hands full as he wrestled it into place.

Riley could grab the gun while he was distracted – that was her plan.

It was now or never.

"Your dad was asking for you," Jesse threw her off focus.

"I'll get him the ambulance," Riley exhaled as she coiled into a sprinter's pose. "I just – I can't let him get away."

"I don't think there's enough time," Jesse knelt down beside her. His lips tightened, searching for the right words. "Riley, it looks bad."

CHAPTER 12

The flights of stairs seemed to stretch on forever, each new level a carbon copy of the one they had just climbed. Riley hadn't paid much attention on her way down the stairwell, but now she was feeling it. The parking garage had somehow doubled in height while she was out on the street.

"If you're lying about this," she panted as they doggedly marched up the steps, "I'm gonna break every bone in your hand."

"Why would I lie?" Jesse slogged on ahead of her.

"Because maybe you're trying to protect Stuart," she glared at the back of his head.

Riley stopped at the next landing, doubling over to massage the burning muscles in her thighs and win back her breath. The stale reek of ancient urine in the confined space wasn't helping.

She exhaled in frustration, angry at the world – angry at herself.

She never asked for any of this.

An asteroid heading for the West Coast?

She should have been at home, eating dinner with her family. She would have welcomed her father's interrogation about her date with Calvin, and her mother insisting that they invite his parents over to meet them next weekend.

But she was here now, in some empty parking garage in the middle of the city, and she had just run all the way down to the ground floor for nothing.

She hadn't found a signal.

She hadn't called an ambulance.

And she had let Sinclair escape.

Riley couldn't believe how quick she had been to take Jesse at his word.

"I guess you won't know for sure until we get to the roof," Jesse huffed at the top of the next flight of stairs, looking back at her while thumbing at a stitch in his side. "Come on, it can't be much farther."

Riley straightened up and set her foot on the next step, willing herself to push through the cramped muscles in her legs as they resumed the never-ending climb.

The stairwell did have an end though.

Just two levels up, Jesse held the door open for her.

She stumbled through, gratefully gasping in lungfuls of fresh air after having endured the stench of the dank crypt.

Dusk was already beginning to settle in over Redhurst, wreathing the cityscape with scattered orange clouds scudding across the western horizon, while the streetlamps below glowed against the deepening purple hues of the approaching evening.

Jesse let the stairwell's door slam shut, jerking Riley out of the tranquil moment.

"Riley?" Susan's voice called across the parking lot. "Come quick."

She staggered across the concrete expanse in disbelief, the

sight of Nolan Armstrong lying underneath a thermal sleeping bag swimming in her vision.

His face was pale.

His lips were blue.

His stomach was unnaturally swollen, the rapidly rising and falling bulge visible – even underneath both layers of the sleeping bag.

Susan was kneeling beside him, holding his hand as she wept silent tears.

Keith Bowman sat with his back against the black pickup truck's rear wheel, blankly staring into the distance, his hands covered in dried blood.

"You said he was gonna be okay!" Riley screamed, running to her father's side.

"We did everything we could," Susan sniffled, wiping her eyes.

"Is that Riley?" Nolan lolled his head towards her, reaching his arm out from underneath the sleeping bag.

"I'm here, Dad," she knelt by his side, taking his hand in hers. He was cold to the touch. She looked up at her mother. "We need to get him to the hospital!"

"We already tried," Susan smiled sadly, glancing over at Keith.

"Well, try again!" Riley wrapped her father's arm around her shoulders and tried to lift him up.

He bellowed in agony, barely an inch off the ground.

"Bullet hit his spleen," Keith croaked in defeat as she laid him back down again. "He's bleeding internally. We can't move him without making it worse."

"But we can't just let him die!" Riley sobbed, looking from her mother to Keith and back to her father.

All three of them had already accepted his fate.

"Whole city's panicking," Nolan panted between pained gasps, "There's no guarantee – anyone's waiting for us – at the hospital."

Riley swallowed as she realized that the only reason her father had been relatively unscathed every time he had been shot in the line of duty was because there were always experienced medical staff just one call away.

And the only person who might have been able to pull the bullet out – Doctor Sinclair – had been the same person who had put the bullet in him.

"What should we do?" tears streamed down her face, some-how already knowing that if there was anything else that they could have done, they would have done it by now.

She mentally kicked herself for running off on some stupid half-cocked revenge quest when she should have been up here, staying by her father's side in his final moments.

"Take care of your mother," Nolan whispered feebly, "Stay safe. Get to Nebraska."

He began shaking, his cold hand squeezing Riley's as a slow smile began to stretch across his stubbled jaw, and he let out a low chuckle.

"Why the hell are you laughing?" she couldn't help but smile back at him, despite the tears rolling down her cheeks.

"Because," he coughed with a grin, "At least I don't have to see your Aunt Lorraine."

CHAPTER 13

She kept waiting for him to wake up.

Nolan Armstrong seemed so peaceful that he could have been sleeping.

Riley remembered the times that she would catch her father sprawled out on the living room couch some mornings – after he had worked the night shift – too exhausted to climb up the stairs to sleep in his own bed.

She would watch him while eating breakfast before going to school. He would sometimes jerk with fits and starts, his subconscious mind reliving some tense moment from his shift that had stuck with him, following him home to haunt him in his sleep.

But this time, a faint smile was creasing the corners of his mouth.

Whatever dream he was having, it was a good one.

She studied his face for movement. Even if she could see just the slightest facial tic, it would have made her heart leap.

But the only thing that stirred now was the early evening breeze fingering through his hair.

The nearby sound of water splashing onto the parking

garage's concrete jerked Riley out of her trance, and she looked up to see Keith Bowman washing the blood off his hands as Jesse upended a bottle for him.

"Susan, we've gotta keep moving," Keith dug at the dried blood between his calluses and underneath his fingernails. "We can't stay here."

Susan didn't answer him.

She simply stared at the thermal sleeping bag draped over her husband's body, idly stroking his cold hand with her thumb, refusing to let go.

"We're not leaving him here," Riley's voice was taut with sudden anger.

She hated everyone.

She hated Keith for bringing them up to the parking garage's roof.

She hated her mother for telling Stuart and Karen that the asteroid was coming.

She hated Jesse for being fucking Jesse.

She hated herself.

Her father wouldn't have been hit by the stray bullet if he hadn't been hugging her.

It was almost unbearable to even think about how much she just wanted to hug her father again, because their last hug had gotten him killed.

"I never said we'd leave him," Keith approached slowly, crouching beside Nolan's body to unzip the sleeping bag. "He's coming with us. We'll find a good place to bury him."

Bury him – the words punched Riley square in the chest.

She struggled to her feet and staggered away, drawing deep breaths as she reeled back towards the red suburban.

"Dad," Jesse called as he cleared space in the back of the black crew cab pickup. "Do we still need two cars? We could probably fit everything in the truck."

"We're better off with two," Keith's jaw was set as he pulled the unzipped sleeping bag off his fallen partner, spreading it across the ground.

"But we'll use twice as much gas," Jesse jumped down from the truck. "What if we don't have enough to make it to Nebraska?"

"Did you miss the jerry cans in the back?" Keith gently squeezed Susan's shoulder as he braced to lift Nolan's limp body into the open sleeping bag. His whiskey-cured voice strained under the weight, "We've got plenty gas. But if we get stuck or the truck breaks down on the road, we're gonna be on our own."

Riley straightened up beside the red suburban, pulling out her phone to distract herself from the finality of the sleeping bag's *zip*.

Her thumbs tapped at her screen until she was staring down at the photo that she had taken outside the supermarket. She and her father were grinning back up at her, despite the whole country being on the brink of chaos.

He's not dead, she told herself. *He can't be.*

Keith and Jesse were just loading somebody else into the back of the truck.

Riley decided that her father was waiting for them at the farm in Nebraska – probably rubbing his stubbled jaw as he sat in Grandma Eleanor's kitchen, biting his tongue every time Aunt Lorraine needled at him, trapped in his chair by the heat of his coffee.

And he needed rescuing.

Summoning her resolve, Riley pocketed her phone and

cracked the suburban's door open, fresh tears streaming down her face as she leaned in to adjust the driver's seat.

CHAPTER 14

"You know how to use this?" Keith Bowman asked through the passenger side window, standing beside the red suburban.

Susan took one puffy-eyed look at her husband's handgun and nodded in silence.

"Good," Keith ejected the pistol's magazine and cocked back the slide to clear the chamber. "I don't feel right about giving you a gun after..." he sucked his front teeth, looking up at the flashing lights of an airplane soaring across the night sky. "But I can't have you two unarmed."

He reached into the red suburban to open up the glove box, stowing the empty pistol inside. Then, with a wary glance at Susan, he leaned into the car, holding the magazine over the center console.

Doubting that the precaution was even necessary, but nodding her understanding, Riley took the magazine and slotted it into the driver's side door's storage compartment.

"What's the plan?" she started the engine before adjusting the mirrors.

"Well, freeway's out," Keith straightened up again. "If we can work our way through the hills, we can probably use the farm roads on the other side. Can you read a map?"

"On my phone, sure," she checked it for a signal for the umpteenth time.

Still nothing.

"Not what I meant," Keith glanced at his black pickup in contemplation. "Alright, stay close. Gonna try the cemetery roads. Might get tricky. Hit me on the two-way if you need me to slow down."

He took a deep breath and nodded in silence at his own plan, as if he was reassuring himself that they could still do this without Nolan.

They weren't exactly without him though.

Not completely.

Keith avoided looking at the thermal sleeping bag in the cargo bed of his truck as he climbed back into his pickup.

Riley reached down into the center console to check that her father's radio was secure and close at hand.

She didn't know what they were going to run into on the road, but she doubted that it could get any worse.

They spiraled down the corkscrew ramp, the rumble of their engines sounding hollow and melancholy in the near-deserted building, as if invisible caretakers of the empty parking garage had gathered to bid them a somber farewell.

There was no sign of Sinclair's white coupe as they passed underneath the freeway's overpass, but plenty of cars had banked up along the on-ramp again, impatient drivers blaring their horns, as if that would magically clear the way before them.

Riley knew that the people taking the freeway wouldn't be the only ones who were in for a long night.

"You should get some rest," she told her mother as she

kept a steady distance behind Keith's truck. "We might not be stopping until we get to Nebraska."

Susan folded her arms in the passenger seat, bristling at the thought of being sent to sleep by her own daughter, but she didn't argue. She was too exhausted to do anything other than shut her red-rimmed eyes.

Aside from a few nasty collisions and the occasional over-loaded family sedan heading back towards the freeway, the streets of Redhurst were almost empty.

It was as if everyone else had already packed up and left, but not without stopping to pick up what others had left behind, first.

They passed by the shattered windows of commercial store-fronts and ransacked strip malls. Ceiling lights flickered from inside abandoned convenience stores and gas stations, as if the looters had tried to take the electricity with them as well.

Riley hit the central door lock as a pair of silhouettes flitted through the darkness in between a set of glowing streetlamps, disappearing over a fence into a residential area.

She wondered how many people had been waiting for the day that society would implode into lawlessness. People with scores to settle, thirsts to quench and lusts to satisfy, having lived their lives on the fringes or in plain sight for years, burdened by a list of people who had wronged them, whether their tormentors had known it or not.

And they had wholeheartedly seized their opportunity in less than a day.

Screams and gunshots rang out in the distance, echoing eerily in the empty streets.

One neighborhood had a house burning on the corner. Blazing embers flew up into the night as the roof fell in, succumbing to the flames as a lone onlooker whooped and whistled with deranged delight.

They cautiously crossed another intersection at the outer city limits, where the streetlamps stopped and the buildings grew fewer and farther between.

Given the current state of Redhurst, Riley couldn't have been happier to finally reach the winding cemetery roads, as much as she had hated them back when she was a kid.

Other than steep inclines and sharp turns that could flip a stomach, there was nothing to see out in the hills. Even weeds struggled to grow in the barren patches in between the headstones stretching across valleys and crests.

Riley knew that her father's parents were buried somewhere in the many graveyards scattered among the hills, but she didn't know which one specifically, let alone which burial plots.

She followed the meandering taillights of Keith's truck along the slim serpentine route. Her mother was snoring softly, slumped in the passenger seat as her head lolled with each narrow twisting turn.

Riley shot up in the driver's seat, suddenly aware of herself beginning to drift off in the swaying motion. She clicked the car's radio on and spun the volume dial low, taking care not to wake her mother. Surfing the stations, she strained her ears for a newscast.

There was nothing.

There was music, sure.

But no emergency broadcasts.

No talk shows.

Not even an ad break.

It was as if the radio presenters had simply lined up a playlist and left the studio.

Regardless of whether people believed the rumors about the asteroid, nobody was willing to wait around long enough to find out for certain.

CHAPTER 15

"Susan, Riley?" Keith Bowman's voice crackled over the police radio in the center console.

"Riley here," she clicked the walkie with a sidelong glance at her sleeping mother.

"Looks like the freeway's clear enough," he replied, the black pickup's taillights glowing red as he slowed down. "I'm thinking we jump on here before the road turns back out again."

The clock was approaching midnight now, with the moon soaring high in the sky.

They had been pushing hard for the past few hours, driving along intermittent lengths of asphalt, gravel and dirt roads scored with the treads of tractor tires.

Every now and then, the farm road would run parallel with the freeway, before steadily growing farther apart again. There were no designated access roads to connect the two routes, other than the faint ruts where the local rural drivers had carved their own paths over the years.

Convertibles, sports cars and luxury sedans lined the grassy embankment, their occupants forced to abandon their vehicles and travel on foot. The appeal of a low ground clearance car might have been a popular trend in the suburban sprawl of Redhurst, but it had no practical value out in the Californian countryside.

Riley snorted at the cruel irony of the luxury car owners escaping the chaotic city streets, bypassing the congested traffic via quiet country roads, only to snag their undercarriage on the slight incline of a small cross-country on-ramp.

She sincerely hoped that Sinclair was among the drivers who had been forced to walk along the side of the freeway, but she couldn't see any sign of his white coupe in the darkness.

"This looks like a good spot," Keith's voice came through the police radio again, his black pickup nosing into a trail of flattened grass.

The contents of the truck's cargo bed shook violently as all four wheels kicked up loose dirt and tufts of grass. Clouds of dust mingled with plumes of exhaust smoke, obscuring the back of the pickup as the haze drifted across the beams of Riley's headlights.

"No sweat," Keith's voice crackled again as he parked along the gravel shoulder of the freeway. "You want me to –"

Riley hit the gas, launching the red suburban up the grassy embankment and hurling their suitcases and buckets of supplies against the rear window.

Their front wheels found purchase on the gravel shoulder, yanking them across the freeway with the sudden traction.

Her foot stomped on the brake pad just as they reached the far lane, jerking her mother awake in the passenger seat.

"No, I think I got it," she breathed victoriously into the walkie.

"Riley, look out!" Susan slapped her daughter's shoulder, eyes wide with horror as she pointed at something in the driver's side window.

The bass-filled boom of a long-haul truck's air horn thundered along the freeway, the blazing beams of its headlights looming larger with each passing moment.

Riley's breath caught in her throat.

Her eyes filled with the array of yellow lights adorning the truck's grille and cabin.

Both Keith and Jesse were yelling profanities through the police radio.

Riley's first thought was to unbuckle her seatbelt before the truck could plow through the side of their suburban, but her thumb fumbled with the release.

Susan Armstrong sprang into action.

Ripping her seatbelt off, she shifted the gearstick into reverse.

Ducking underneath the steering wheel, she shoved Riley's foot off the brake pad and slammed the accelerator with her fist.

Riley came back to her senses just as they crunched over the gravel shoulder, pumping the brakes before they could careen backwards down the grassy embankment again.

The suburban's engine revved impotently against the locked-up tires as the long hauler roared past, the truck driver reaching across his cabin to flip the bird out the window.

The two women panting hard in the silence, Susan took her hand off the accelerator and slowly sat upright in the passenger seat again.

"Are you two done giving us a fucking heart attack?" Keith's breathing was just as labored.

"We're good," Susan snatched up the police radio, staring sidelong at Riley. "I think it's about time we switched drivers though."

"You and me both," Keith replied over the sound of a car door's slam.

"Come on," Susan reached for her door handle, "Your turn to sleep."

Riley held up a hand, furrowing her eyebrows and straining her ears.

A voice floated through the night air.

She looked over at Keith's black pickup and reached for the walkie.

"Are you guys still in the truck?" she thumbed the two-way.

The voice came again, closer this time.

"Just looking for my protein bars," Keith crackled over the sound of rustling upholstery, "Jesse, did you move – "

Something heavy smacked into the side of their suburban, and Riley threw up her arms, expecting a shower of broken glass and shredded metal.

It took a moment for her to realize that they hadn't been T-boned by another vehicle.

Confused, she glanced at her side mirror to see the shape of a man trying the rear door handle, finding it locked.

"Let us in!" he growled, banging the window with the flat of his hand.

Riley's heart skipped a beat and she fumbled for the gearstick, kicking it into drive before gunning the engine and fishtailing out onto the freeway.

"MOVE, MOVE, MOVE!!" she screamed into the walkie, looking up at the rearview to see the would-be hitchhiker rushing towards Keith's idling pickup instead, followed by a handful of sprinting silhouettes. She stared at the truck, "WHY AREN'T THEY MOVING!?"

Shit, Riley realized that she hadn't clicked the talk button on the two-way.

"What's going on?" Keith's tires crunched over the gravel shoulder as he pulled out onto the freeway, following their lead.

He was too late though – the stowaway had already jumped up into the truck's cargo bed.

"Give me the ammo!" Susan reached into the glove box for the pistol.

Keeping her eyes on the road, Riley's fingers scrabbled in her door's storage compartment, searching for the magazine.

Her fingertips traced the top of it just as Keith's pickup roared past in the next lane, the unexpected passenger crouching in the cargo bed and clutching onto the side rail for dear life.

Riley caught hold of the magazine and tossed it into her mother's lap.

Susan rammed it home and thumbed the pistol's slide release before winding down the window.

The gun barked as she switched hands, blasting a hole into the dashboard.

"Oh!" Susan jumped in her seat, taking her finger off the trigger and glancing sidelong at her daughter before pointing the barrel out the window. "Get us up alongside them!"

Riley's heart was pounding in her chest, barely able to hold the steering wheel steady with all of the adrenaline pumping through her veins.

She was pushing the suburban to its absolute limits when Keith tapped his brakes up ahead, prying the stowaway's fingers loose as the man lurched towards the truck cab's rear window.

Keith hit the accelerator again, and the man staggered backwards in the cargo bed, stumbling over something as the rushing wind caught him off guard, sending him tumbling out the back of the pickup to catch a face full of asphalt.

Riley swerved halfway into the next lane to avoid the would-be hitchhiker's flailing limbs as he rolled across the freeway, his body bouncing high before skidding to a stop in her rearview mirror.

Susan flipped the safety lever on the pistol and threw it back into the glove box, her hands trembling with unspent energy as she reached over her shoulder for the strap of her seatbelt.

"You see that shit!?" Keith cheered through the two-way, ecstatic with the result. "Let's hold off on switching drivers for a minute."

Riley's hands were glued to the steering wheel.

She couldn't pick up the walkie to reply even if she wanted to.

CHAPTER 16

"Alright, I think we've put enough distance behind us," Keith Bowman's voice crackled through the police radio. "There's a rest stop up ahead."

Riley was hesitant to slow down after their last run-in.

She wasn't tired.

They could keep going for a few more hours, just to be sure.

In the wired state that she was in, she could probably drive all the way to Nebraska.

"We'll see you in a minute," Susan Armstrong clicked the walkie and looked sidelong at her daughter. "I need to use the bathroom."

Reluctantly, Riley slowed down and took the exit after Keith's black crew cab pickup. The loss of speed made it feel as though they were crawling across the concrete parking lot.

A solitary truck and a gray motorhome stood like silent sentinels beside the bathroom block at the other end of the quiet rest stop.

Keith stopped at the halfway point of the parking lot, pulling the pickup lengthways across three car spaces.

"How you guys doing for gas?" he asked as his taillights

switched off.

"Still got half a tank," Riley glanced at the dashboard as she pulled up behind his truck.

"Good," his voice came back as the pickup's doors opened, him and Jesse climbing out. Keith was holding his shotgun in one hand and his radio in the other. "Speaking of tanks," he jerked his head towards the bathroom block, "Ladies first?"

Susan was the first to accept the invitation, swinging the passenger side door open and setting foot on the concrete. She paused for a moment, glancing sidelong at Riley before cracking open the glove box and sliding Nolan's handgun into her waistband at the small of her back.

Riley's legs and back rejoiced as she stretched beside the red suburban.

Allowing herself the brief moment of bliss, she stopped to lock the doors, picking up on her mother's sense of caution.

"Just a quick pit stop," Keith said as he climbed up into the back of his truck, checking the cargo bed's contents after the unexpected passenger had made a mess of things. "We'll see if we can find a gas station somewhere up the road. Don't wanna tap into the reserves just yet."

"Is Nolan okay?" Susan paused beside the pickup, peering at the zipped-up thermal sleeping bag.

"Could be better," Keith stooped to lay the sleeping bag flat, "Think he might've had something to do with tripping up that asshole back there."

"That was some good driving," Jesse remarked as Riley walked past.

"Thanks," was all she gave back, brushing him off.

What else does he want me to say? Riley thought to herself as she and her mother passed the front of the pickup. *My dad taught me? I'm not going there. Not with him.*

The truck and the motorhome stood on either side of the concrete lot, both of them rumbling with bearlike snores from within.

Cars and trucks flew past the rest stop, probably more than usual for this side of midnight, but nothing close to the start-stop traffic of Redhurst.

With each set of passing headlights, Riley caught flashes of the parking lot's stark emptiness, broken only by a few lonely desert shrubs dotting the side of the road.

The high-pitched howls of a pack of coyotes calling in the distance drove Riley and Susan into the rest stop's bathroom faster than their urge to use the facilities.

Inside was nothing special, despite being the only building for dozens of miles. Moths droned lazily around flickering fluorescent lights, illuminating a pair of bathroom stalls opposite a single sink and mirror.

"You first," Susan checked both stalls before retreating to the entrance. "I'll watch the door."

Riley was surprised to find half a jumbo roll of toilet paper inside, given that there was no sign of regular maintenance in the rest of the bathroom, every surface covered in a thin layer of grime.

"Were you really gonna shoot that guy on the freeway?" she perched on the seat, staring up at the cobwebs in the ceiling.

"If it came down to it," Susan answered quietly. "I'm glad that I didn't have to, but yes, I would've."

"It's only been one day and we're already killing people," Riley finished up and flushed.

"People will do anything when they're desperate," Susan waited for her to wash up before handing her the pistol. Holding her daughter's gaze, she added, "Who knows how long that man was waiting on the side of the road? If he had a gun, he wouldn't have hesitated to kill the both of us for what we have. Don't give me that look, you know it's true. He had his group to take care of, just like we have ours."

Susan disappeared into the bathroom stall, and Riley stared down at the gun in her hands, wondering if she could really kill a stranger.

She could kill Sinclair – no problem – but that was justified.

Someone who was just trying to hitch a ride though, that was different.

"Riley, you need to underst–"

"I get it," she hated the idea, but she wasn't stupid. If it truly was kill or be killed, she would rather choose the former, but she didn't have to like it. "What I don't get is... why was Keith laughing about it after?"

The policeman had been on the verge of a breakdown on the roof of the parking garage after running down one of those looters in the city, but he was practically on cloud nine after he had thrown the hitchhiker off the back of his truck.

"It's... complicated," Susan flushed and opened up the bathroom stall. Crossing over to the sink and gazing up at Riley's reflection in the grimy mirror, she pursed her lips, poising to offer an explanation before deciding against it. "Look, just be happy that he's on our side."

Riley handed her the pistol as they headed back outside, the traffic slightly heavier along the freeway. They passed by Keith and Jesse alongside the motorhome, with Riley's eyes fixed on the red suburban.

Her stomach rumbled as she took the keys out of her pocket. She had forgotten to eat.

All of them had.

The loss of her father coupled with the mad rush to get out of Redhurst had robbed her of her appetite, but now she felt like she could devour a three-course meal and come back for seconds.

She couldn't crack the trunk open fast enough, her hunger driving her actions now. She thrust her hand into the bucket of fruit and pulled up the first thing she touched – the kitchen knife. She laid it back down gently and reached into the bucket again.

Almost ripping a banana in half, she peeled it in three seconds and wolfed it in two, with Susan biting a chunk out of an apple beside her, just as hungry.

Riley was picking out a sandwich spread while her mother twisted the tab off a bag of bread, when a pair of headlights washed across the parking lot behind them.

Susan dropped the apple from her mouth back into the bucket, nudged Riley to one side and shut the trunk.

They turned and shielded their eyes with one arm as the glaring headlights approached.

"Y'all ladies wouldn't happen to have somethin' to eat, would ye?" a tattooed arm hung out of the brown station wagon's driver's side window, the man's face wreathed in shadow.

"We didn't have enough time to pack before we left," Susan had her free hand resting on the hilt of the pistol tucked in her waistband at the small of her back. "We were hoping to find something on the road."

"Slim pickin's too, huh?" his fingers drummed the side of his door. The silhouette of his face turned towards Keith's truck, "Must be every diner 'n' fast food joint from here to Cali done run outta food or closed up shop."

"Ask her what's in the back," a woman's voice piped up in the passenger seat, the end of her cigarette glowing as she took a quick puff.

"What y'all got in the trunk, there?" the lower half of his face materialized as he peered out the window, a silver tooth glinting in between his scruffy mustache and beard.

"We were just checking on our dog," Riley quickly made up an excuse. "He's been growling a lot since we left."

The silver tooth disappeared as he began whispering with his passenger.

Riley swallowed, exchanging a nervous glance with her mother.

"Looks like y'all in luck," he pulled the brown station wagon over and switched off the engine. "I'm a vet. Maybe I can take a look."

He cracked the door open and stepped out.

Riley hated judging a book by its cover, but the man looked nothing like an animal doctor.

Dressed in a sweat-stained singlet and sagging shorts, he had tattoos covering both arms, from shoulder to wrist, with a spider web across his neck and a black teardrop beneath one of his eyes.

The woman emerging from the passenger side had a scar across her cheek. Her hair was a tangled cobweb of black and gray, with edgy eyes darting between Riley and Susan as she took a shaky draw of her cigarette.

"Sure, he's off his leash though," Riley reached for the trunk's release before pausing, "And I should probably warn you, he *really* doesn't like strangers."

"Especially vets," Susan added, clenching the pistol's grip.

"Go 'head, then," his silver tooth gleamed as he called them on their bluff, "I seen plenty bad dogs."

"And bitches," the scar-cheeked woman circled around the back of the station wagon.

"Get back!" Susan whipped the pistol out, aiming the barrel at the tattooed spider web. "Or we'll be the last bitches you'll ever see."

"Whoa now," he grinned, holding his hands up, "I ain't been nothin' but nice to y'all."

"They're lying," the woman blew a plume of smoke before creeping forward. "They got food."

Riley glanced back at the kitchen knife through the rear window of the suburban's trunk, but it was useless to her now.

Improvising, she ripped the set of keys from the lock and closed her hand around the ring, two keys jutting out from her fist as she squared up against the scar-cheeked woman.

Flicking her cigarette across the parking lot, the woman pulled out a switchblade.

"Yeah, we got food," Keith Bowman appeared around the front of the suburban, his shotgun barrel pointed at the tattooed man's torso. "We got shells too. Ask me real nice, and I'll fill that empty stomach right up."

"We ain't mean no harm, sir," the silver-toothed man swallowed, his grin disappearing. "My uncle told us to meet him here. We just tryin' to get out the state, same as y'all."

"Bullshit," now it was Riley's turn to call him on his bluff.

"I swear," he nodded towards the gray motorhome parked beside the bathroom block. "Y'all could go ask him."

"Go ask him yourself," Keith's shotgun jerked sharply before tracing the tattooed man's every step, ready to explode at the slightest change in pace. He spoke over his shoulder, "Jesse, get behind the wheel."

Riley and Susan waited until the scar-cheeked woman passed into Keith's line of sight before splitting up around the sides of the suburban, with Riley taking the passenger seat.

Keith climbed back into the pickup once the pair of thugs reached the motorhome on the other end of the parking lot.

"Susan, you take point," his voice crackled through the police radio. "Jesse's taking over. Let's get back on the road."

"We're just gonna let them go!?" Riley clicked the two-way, staring sidelong at Susan as she started up the engine.

"Save the ammo," Keith replied as they passed by in the suburban, the pickup pulling out behind them. "We're gonna need it down the road."

"What about whoever's in the motorhome?" Riley peered at the two desperados standing beside the side door.

The tattooed man's silver tooth gleamed back at her as he gave them a wave.

The scar-cheeked woman was hunched over the door handle, her switchblade catching the flickering fluorescent light from the bathroom block as she tried to pick the lock.

Riley furrowed her eyebrows, her gaze shifting between the radio and her mother.

Susan simply pursed her lips and shook her head, keeping her eyes on the road.

Exhaling in frustration, Riley reached across the center console and blared the horn, hoping to wake up the sleeping occupants.

"Not our people," Keith's voice came back as they pulled out onto the freeway. "Not our problem."

CHAPTER 17

They weren't moving.

Why weren't they moving?

"Dad?" Riley Armstrong rubbed at her bleary eyes and sat up in the passenger seat.

Her eardrums popped as she yawned, and she glanced around the car.

The engine was off, the keys were gone, and there was no sign of her parents.

She choked as she remembered that her father wouldn't answer.

Of course he wouldn't.

She had hoped that it had all been part of some terrible nightmare.

Grisly flashbacks flew unbidden into her mind – her father collapsing onto the concrete, the gun rattling in Sinclair's hand, and the finality of the thermal sleeping bag's *zip*.

Riley squinted against the sunlight pouring in through the windshield. They weren't in the middle of the desert anymore. Grassy plains stretched into the distance, broken only by the slight bumps of low hills on the horizon.

She must have slept all the way to Wyoming.

Blinking hard, she took another look around at the landscape.

They weren't even on the freeway anymore.

Were they lost?

"Mom?" she unbuckled her seatbelt, looking over at the empty driver's seat.

Her pupils dilated as she caught movement in the side mirror, and she ducked down in her seat, her dry mouth swallowing a wave of black dread as she realized that all of the car's doors were unlocked.

"... gonna let her sleep," Susan Armstrong's voice pierced through the panic.

Riley breathed a sigh of relief and she opened up the passenger door.

Almost immediately, a stiff gust of wind buffeted her ears and whipped her hair across her face.

"Look who's up," Keith looked over his shoulder as he tipped a jerry can into the suburban's fuel tank.

"Well, that certainly changes things," Susan put one hand on her hip with a glad smile. "Come on, let's eat. You're driving after lunch."

Keith shut the fuel hatch and followed Riley and Susan back towards his black crew cab pickup, where Jesse was busy making sandwiches in the front passenger seat.

"Why are we so far away?" Riley looked down the road, seeing the freeway running perpendicular in the distance.

"If anybody saw us gassing up," Keith stowed his jerry can underneath a tarpaulin with the other three reserve containers, tying the canvas down securely, "We'd be dead before we got the fuel caps back on."

"It's not that bad, is it?" she asked as they climbed up into

93

the truck, pulling hard to shut the door against the stubborn wind. "What about the gas stations?"

"Bone dry," Jesse buttered up two slices of bread and slapped a slice of deli meat in between them.

"Everybody's filling up," Keith snatched up a sandwich and took a mouthful, frowning as he chewed. "Most places look like rush hour in downtown Redhurst – just a cluster-fuck of parking lots with a whole lot of yelling and not a whole lot of moving."

"Those were the good ones," Jesse passed a pair of sandwiches to Riley and Susan sitting in the cluttered backseat. "The bad ones... let's just say guns aren't a great idea around the pumps."

Riley had her sandwich raised halfway up to her mouth when her mother grabbed her wrist.

"Do you have a fridge in here, Keith?" Susan glanced around at the tangle of cardboard boxes, empty plastic wrappers and musty smelling clothes.

It was impossible to be certain by sight alone.

"I'm not driving a damn limous–"

Susan snatched the sandwich out of Riley's hand, cranked the window open and threw both meals out into the wind.

"Well, that was a waste of food," Jesse scowled at the culmination of his culinary prowess flying away in the side mirror's reflection.

Keith Bowman chewed for a moment longer before glowering sidelong at his son, cracking the door open and leaning outside to cough up his mouthful.

"Like vinegar, right?" Susan asked knowingly.

"Like shit dipped in shit," Keith washed his mouth out with a bottle of water.

"Didn't you check the meat first?" Riley accused Jesse, her appetite leaving the truck.

"I thought it was just condensation or something," he opened up his sandwich to reveal a glistening film of white slime across the surface. "How long does deli meat normally last outside the fridge?"

"I wouldn't touch it after the first hour," Susan folded her arms, keeping the window open to let the truck air out. "They don't call them cold cuts for nothing. I think we're gonna eat in our car."

Riley gladly stepped out.

Between the smell of the spoiled ham sandwiches and the pickup's cabin itself, she was all too happy to eat peanut butter and jelly in the suburban instead.

As she savored the nutty sweet sandwiches, they reminded her of lazy after-school snacks with her father, and she swallowed sadly, wishing that he was here.

She suddenly didn't want to be on the side of the highway anymore.

Starting up the ignition, Riley looked up and down the road before spinning the steering wheel, heading back towards the freeway.

"Looks like we're moving again," Keith's voice came over the radio as the pickup's wheels spun in the rearview mirror. "Thanks for the heads-up."

"Is everything okay, Riley?" Susan asked around her mouthful as she buckled up her seatbelt, looking back over her shoulder to check that Keith and Jesse weren't too far behind.

"Just peachy," Riley kept her eyes on the road, "Let's just get there."

"Alright, we're heading east though," Susan pointed out the

correct on-ramp before picking up the walkie. "Keith, we're gonna take the lead until the next stop."

"Yeah, no shit," his voice crackled back.

"I just need a few hours and I can take over again," Susan settled into the passenger seat as they jumped back onto the freeway. "Let me know when, okay?"

Riley grunted as her mother drifted off to sleep.

The road was clear as far as the horizon.

She supposed that they had gotten in front of the traffic overnight, although the thought left her as soon as they came across the first gas station, filled with cars and vans and trucks that were either caught up in the congestion or abandoned with empty gas tanks.

Distant mountains rose and fell in her peripherals as the mile markers flashed past, one grassy plain indistinguishable from the next grassy plain. She could have been driving along a gigantic treadmill if it hadn't been for the occasional vehicle pulled over on the shoulder, discarded relics of drivers who had fallen victim to a lack of fuel.

It was mid-afternoon by the time they reached a forested valley, with pine trees growing thick on either side. It was almost as if all of the trees across the entire state of Wyoming had picked up their roots and gathered into one place.

Up ahead was another cluster of sedans and suburbans that had been abandoned along the side of the road. A food delivery truck had its rear hatch rolled up, with only stacks of empty wooden pallets inside.

Riley was scanning the scattered cars for Sinclair's white coupe when a volley of eggs soared over the freeway's concrete divider, cracking open across the suburban's windshield.

"What the *hell!?*" Riley instinctively flicked on the wipers, which only served to distort the glass even further with the smeared egg yolks.

She nudged the brake pad, searching for the police radio in the center console to let Keith know, when she caught a glimpse of an orange car up ahead, parked lengthways across the lanes.

"BRAKE!!" she screamed into the walkie as her tires screeched across the freeway, jerking her mother awake just in time for the inertia to fling them both against their seatbelts.

"Riley, what's —"

Susan's startled shout was cut short as Keith's pickup plowed into the back of the suburban.

Riley's teeth snapped shut as her head jolted back and forth in the whiplash.

Glass crystals rained all around them as the locked-up tires skidded along the asphalt.

"Ugh, my head," she fought the urge to hurl. "Who the fuck —"

"Riley, language," Susan chided her in a daze, her hand brushing shards of broken glass as she groggily tried to sit upright.

With doubled vision, Riley peered through the cracked and murky windshield to see the shape of an orange vintage muscle car up ahead.

Her scrambled thoughts drifted to wondering where she had seen the vehicle before, when a series of strained shouts erupted from Keith's truck behind them.

She looked up at the twisted rearview mirror to see Jesse slapping his father and punching the airbags as a group of people jumped over the freeway's concrete divider.

Swallowing her nausea, Riley unbuckled her seatbelt and tugged at the glove box, but it wouldn't budge.

"Shit, shit, shit, shit, shit!" Riley pulled and wrenched at the glove box's handle until it snapped off. She held up the piece of plastic in disbelief before slamming the dashboard with her fist, "Piece of shit!"

As if she had hit an emergency button, the compartment popped open.

Riley's lower back groaned in agony as she leaned over to reach for her father's handgun cradled in the far corner of the glove box.

She managed to brush the grip with her fingertips when a young man's voice floated into the car.

"Too slow," he taunted her through the passenger side's broken window.

Gritting her teeth as she defied the sharp pain in her neck, Riley turned to see a broken wooden plank poking in through the window frame, its jagged edge pointing menacingly at the soft flesh of her dazed mother's throat.

CHAPTER 18

"Get off me!" Riley gasped through gritted teeth as a pair of rough hands attempted to haul her out of the ruined suburban.

Broken glass crystals poured from her lap as a thin man wearing a trucker's cap reached in and swung her feet out over the asphalt.

He grabbed her shirt next, and she batted away one of his hands, but the other caught hold of her wrist and yanked her down to the ground, a sharp twinge in her pelvis sending an electrical bolt of fiery pain up a cluster of nerves in her lower back.

She groaned in agony on her hands and knees among the glass shards in the middle of the freeway when the trucker bent over her, one hand seizing her by the hair.

"Wait, wait, wait, my neck!" Riley pleaded, her stiff neck still throbbing from the whiplash as she struggled to her feet.

He grabbed her by the upper arm instead, none too gently, and dragged her staggering past Keith's black pickup, where Susan and Jesse were already kneeling on the ground with their hands up.

The same guy who had threatened to pierce Susan's throat

with the broken plank of wood was now holding Nolan's handgun, walking in a slow circle around their apparent prisoners as the rest of his college-aged friends searched the vehicles.

They looked like the stereotypical privileged kids of Southern California.

Riley had spent most of her early years at school trying to fit in with them, but as she grew older, she had learned that her life was far easier when she simply avoided them.

They were only a few years older than Riley, dressed as if they were heading to the beach – visibly bitter and out of place in the windy land-locked state of Wyoming.

Dressed more appropriately – but odd company among his companions – was the trucker, whose jacket was embroidered with *Merle*. Middle-aged and gaunt, he threw Riley to the ground alongside her mother.

"You don't have to do anything stupid," Susan Armstrong's eyes were on the guy with the pistol as she attempted to negotiate with their ambushers. "Just take what we have and go."

"Yeah, that's the plan," he sneered, sharing a chuckle with Merle as a pair of his friends rummaged through the contents of the black pickup's cargo bed, "Hayden, what's the hold up?"

"He's a heavy son of a bitch," another young man appeared around the side of the truck, hunched over as he dragged Keith Bowman's limp body towards the others.

"What did you do to him!?" Riley shouted angrily at the sight of the gash across Keith's forehead.

"I didn't do anything," Hayden huffed, straightening up with a frown, "That's what he gets for not wearing a seatbelt."

Jesse swallowed, nodding sidelong at Riley.

In the back of the pickup, a pair of blondes – a guy and a

girl, similar enough to be siblings – coughed and covered their noses as they reeled away from something in the cargo bed.

"There's a body back here!" the guy jumped over the side rail, helping his sister down.

"So dump it," the one holding the pistol shrugged. "What else is in the–"

"Don't you dare touch my husband!" Susan struggled to her feet as Hayden climbed up into the back of the truck.

"You don't get a choice," Merle halted her before she could take two steps, planting his hand on her chest while the guy with the gun kicked at the back of her knee and pistol-whipped her over the head.

"You fucking prick!" Riley's back tweaked with pain again before she could even put one foot on the ground.

"Shaun, are you out of your mind?" the blonde girl put herself between him and Susan, checking the back of her head as she moaned in pain.

"Whatever," he turned the handgun on Riley and Jesse, daring them to make a move as Hayden dropped Nolan Armstrong's body over the side of the pickup, the thermal sleeping bag thudding onto the asphalt. Shaun glanced over at Merle, "You, go check if the truck still works."

"We got water back here!" Hayden tossed bottles down to Merle and the blonde guy as they walked over to the front of the pickup. Hayden dug around some more, untying the tarpaulin before holding up one of the jerry cans. "And we got gas!"

"Fuck yes," Shaun jerked his gaze away from Riley and Jesse. "Go fill up my car."

As Hayden jumped down, Jesse subtly began nudging his knocked-out father, trying to rouse him, while Susan – dazed and disoriented – crawled on her stomach towards her hus-

101

band's body.

Hearing her mother's meek moans of anguish filled Riley with anger.

Despite the throbbing pain in her neck and back, she inched forward while Shaun was distracted, heart pounding as she coiled to make a lunge for the pistol.

Just as she was calculating the distance to his hand, he stepped out of reach to investigate the sound of something plastic dragging along the asphalt towards them.

"What you got there, Katanya?" he asked as a sixth assailant came into view, the ebony girl pulling along a pair of suitcases.

"I thought we could – what the hell did you do?" Katanya dropped the luggage handles and crouched beside Susan and the blonde girl.

"She stepped outta line," Shaun held his arms out wide, as if it was all a game to him, whirling back towards Riley and Jesse with a smarmy grin on his face. "I had to make an example outta her before these two got any ideas."

Keith stirred as the pickup's engine rumbled.

His pupils dilated at the sight of Shaun looming over them with a pistol.

Instinctively, Keith reached for his holster, only to find that it was empty, remembering that Sinclair had stolen his handgun.

"Look who just joined the party," Shaun pointed the gun at Keith, noticing the taser and pepper spray on his hip, "Undo your belt. You a cop?"

"Is it that obvious?" he asked sarcastically, tossing his police kit belt aside, his badge glinting in the mid-afternoon sun.

"You're from Redhurst," Shaun tilted his head to one side to read the emblem before glancing back at the black pickup. "You know, I think we were following you outta the city. You stopped just before the freeway though. What happened?"

"I should've kept going," Keith muttered on his knees, his gaze dropping to his partner's body in the sleeping bag. "Fucking got my best friend killed."

Riley felt a pang of pity for the man as she caught tears welling in the corners of his eyes. She had been too wrapped up in her own grief to acknowledge that Keith was hurting too.

"Yeah, you *really* should've kept going," there wasn't a trace of sympathy in Shaun's voice. "Maybe you could've been throwing eggs with the rest of us at the next cars to pass by." He jerked his head towards the sleeping bag, "Now, you're gonna have to join your friend here."

"You're gonna kill them?" Katanya whirled around and rose to her feet. "He's a cop!"

"Yeah, that's kinda why we have to," Shaun frowned and smiled at the same time, as if it was all so obvious. "If it was just these three, I'd let them go. Probably. But *he's* gonna come after us."

"Let me give you something to think about," Keith held his hands up, offering no resistance. "If you kill us like this – on our knees, unarmed and complying – you're gonna regret it. We won't physically come after you, sure. But I promise you, we're gonna follow you everywhere, for the rest of your life."

"This wasn't part of the plan, Shaun," the blonde girl looked up from Susan, "Imagine if it was us in their place!"

"You should listen to your friends," Keith began in a measured tone, "Look, here's what we can –"

"I'm the one with the gun, remember?" Shaun cut off whatever compromise Keith was about to offer. "I don't have to listen to anyone."

"You don't have to kill us!" Riley burst out, making eye

contact with Keith, "We're just trying to survive, same as you." Then, without even realizing it, Keith's words from back at the rest stop came pouring out of her mouth, "You should save the ammo. You're gonna need it down the road."

"You know, you're probably right," Shaun admitted as Hayden reappeared around the side of the black crew cab pickup, tossing an empty jerry can into the truck's cargo bed. "We should save the ammo. Hayden, go grab that broken plank for me."

"Wait," Katanya shuffled over to the pair of suitcases as Hayden disappeared again. "Tell us the codes for your luggage first."

"Just shoot the locks off," Riley looked away sullenly, realizing that she had just sentenced them to slow splintery deaths rather than the mercy of quick clean bullets.

"We need warmer clothes," Katanya locked eyes with Shaun before turning back to the three on their knees. "We'll let you live if you tell us. All of you."

"Bullshit," Riley stared at Hayden as he returned with the broken wooden plank.

"9–1–1," Susan drew herself up on her knees, brushing the blonde girl's hand away and gently touching the tender spot on the back of her head where she had been pistol-whipped. "That's my code."

Riley's eyebrows furrowed at her mother, her head cocking slightly, disappointed that she wasn't putting up more of a fight.

"They're just clothes, Riley," Susan sensed her daughter's frustration. "We can find some more."

Riley looked up at Katanya, then sidelong at Keith and Jesse. If the college girl really was offering to let them live, then she supposed that it was at least worth trying.

What do we have to gain by resisting anyway? Riley reasoned with herself. *They waste one bullet busting open the lock?*

"4–2–0," she reluctantly gave up her suitcase's code, avoiding Susan's curious gaze.

"That was easy," Shaun chuckled, holding his other hand out for the broken wooden plank from Hayden. "Guess they're useless to us alive now."

"You piece of –"

"You owe us!" Jesse cut across Riley, finally finding his voice. "We led you outta the city when everything was falling apart. You'd still be stuck in Redhurst if it wasn't for us!"

"He's right," Hayden pulled the broken plank out of Shaun's reach, stepping back and weighing the jagged piece of wood in his hand, simultaneously weighing up his own thoughts. After a moment's contemplation, he turned away and tossed the plank into the forest. "We weren't getting anywhere in traffic until we saw their police lights come on. I kinda feel bad about taking all their shit now."

Shaun eyed each of his friends in turn, all of them banding together against him.

He breathed a deep sigh of disappointment.

"Alright, have it your way," he shrugged, sliding the handgun into his waistband at the small of his back before a scornful grin crept across his face. "I tried to give them an easy way out, but I guess you'd rather have them die slow instead."

"What are you talking about?" Katanya asked as Shaun stooped to pick up Keith's police kit belt.

"Pretty simple," he climbed up into the back of the pickup truck and helped Hayden load the suitcases. "Without food, water, or gas, they're not gonna last long out here. Better them than us though."

"Thanks," Susan rose to her feet, staring up at Shaun as he snorted in amusement at her, "For giving us a chance."

"There's a landscaping truck about half a mile back," the blonde girl pointed down the road with a mixture of guilt and pity. "Maybe you can find a shovel to bury your husband."

"He won't be the last dead body you'll have to bury," Shaun jumped down from the pickup's cargo bed, "That's if any of you live long enough to dig another hole."

CHAPTER 19

"Fuck!!" Keith slammed the red suburban's steering wheel as the engine coughed and spluttered and died again. The gash on his head was wrapped with the torn scraps of his undershirt's sleeves, held in place by a bootlace.

Shaun, Katanya, Hayden, Merle and the two blonde siblings were long gone, along with Keith's black pickup and all of their supplies.

"I don't understand, it still has gas," Riley watched the fuel gauge drop back to zero as the dashboard's lights flickered out. One hand holding her throbbing lower back, she skirted around the front of the suburban to where Jesse was leaning over the engine. "Why are you saying it's a fuel issue?"

"Well, it's not the battery," he pulled the dipstick out and inspected the amber-coated tip. "The oil looks good. Nothing's broken underneath. I can't check the spark plugs without a socket wrench, but if the engine's been working fine from yesterday until now, I don't think it's the plugs either. It's gotta be the fuel."

"You think they put something in the tank?" Keith pulled the fuel door lever and unscrewed the cap, peering at the mouth of

107

the filler pipe.

"Probably," Jesse shrugged, releasing the hood prop and closing the lid, "Doesn't take much water to screw up the engine."

"Assholes," Riley exhaled, her mother safely out of earshot somewhere down the road. She frowned and looked back at Jesse, "Hold on, I thought water and oil don't mix? Can't we just drain the tank and fill it back up with just the gas?"

"Your car's cooked," Jesse shook his head as he wiped his greasy hands off on his jeans. "We could probably do it with another car, but we don't have anything to siphon the tank with, or anything to hold the fuel in. Maybe we should look ar–"

"What the fuck were you thinking?" Keith smacked the fuel door shut and glared at Riley, his jaw hardening. "You barely gave me a warning. You just screamed and slammed the brakes."

"I'm sorry," she winced as she turned to face him before massaging her stiff neck. She thought about adding a barb, but her body was aching too much to argue. "I couldn't see anything until it was too late."

"Too late, that's an understatement," he raised his eyebrows in that same patronizing way that Nolan had whenever he wasn't done proving a point. "You need to be aware of your surroundings, at all times. But it's *too late* for that now, isn't it? Because now, we're all fucked!"

"I probably would've done the same thing, Dad," Jesse stood alongside her. "I've never heard of people using eggs to carjack someone. I would've hit the wipers too."

"I'm not surprised – that's that Palmview privilege talking," Keith's stony gaze went from Jesse to Riley and back to Jesse again. "You never should've moved out. You've been sheltered for too long. Both of you. Now you don't know how to handle yourselves when shit hits the fan."

"You're such a fucking hypocrite!" Riley had heard enough, her aching body be damned. "*You* need to be aware of your surroundings. *You* don't know how to handle yourself. Sinclair took *your* gun while *you* were having a breakdown. *You* got my dad killed, and now you're blaming everyone else but yourself for the mess we're in."

Riley would have kept going had it not been for the sharp twinge in the damaged cluster of nerves in her lower back.

She scowled at him instead before limping over to drop down beside the concrete divider, unable to sit down in the red suburban because of all the broken glass scattered across the seats.

Glancing between Riley and Keith, Jesse stuffed his hands into his pockets and took a withdrawn interest in the crushed rear of the suburban.

With Riley's harsh words still echoing in his ears, Keith sucked his front teeth and stared up at the mid-afternoon sky – still a beautiful day despite just how screwed they were.

A steady metallic scrape against the asphalt snapped them all out of their trance, and they turned to see Susan Armstrong marching back up the road with a shovel.

Taking a deep breath, Keith walked over to the thermal sleeping bag and stooped to pick up his fallen partner's body.

They chose a shady spot on a gentle slope, a few dozen yards away from the gravel shoulder of the freeway.

The daylight hours were beginning to wane as Keith and Jesse took turns tossing dirt.

Despite the brooding silence between Riley and Keith, she stood up to help.

"Don't," Susan was lashing together two lengths of wood with handfuls of overgrown grass. "You'll only make it worse."

"Make what worse?" Riley asked, wondering if her mother had sensed the tension.

"Your back," Susan pulled the makeshift twine into a knot, the stubborn lengths of wood falling apart again. She sighed and patted the ground beside her, "Come on, help me with this."

"It's for Dad, I'm not just gonna sit by while they do all the work," Riley sighed, easing herself down all the same.

"You're still doing your part," Susan held out the two pieces of wood. Lowering her voice, she added, "I need you to be able to walk."

"Mom, I can still walk," Riley furrowed her eyebrows as she held the lengths of wood in the shape of a cross.

"For long distances?" Susan pursed her lips before glancing over at Keith and Jesse having a hushed conversation of their own beside the grave. "Riley, we might need to walk to the next town. If they think that we're slowing them down, or we're too much of a burden... they might decide to go on ahead."

"And just leave us behind?" Riley didn't want to believe it, but after the way that she had just chewed out Keith, she wouldn't have been surprised.

"Don't get me wrong," Susan looped and knotted the grass around the makeshift cross, "I have every belief that they'll do everything they can to help us – provided that it's convenient for them. But if the road ahead gets too tough and they have to make a decision, well... we're close, but we're not family."

CHAPTER 20

The sun was hanging low by the time they laid Nolan Armstrong to rest. It was hard to believe that he was even gone. Just yesterday, he had been hugging Riley on the roof of that parking garage... until his arms fell from around her.

Riley had her eyes closed, weeping silent tears.

Part of her was still expecting him to drape his arm over her shoulders, pull her close, and tell her that everything was going to be okay.

But that part of her would have to stay here with him.

She couldn't afford to be sentimental anymore.

Not if she and her mother wanted to make it to their relatives in Nebraska in one piece.

Whatever challenges lay on the road ahead, neither one of them could rely on anyone else to come to their rescue.

"Everything's gonna be okay," Riley said in a choked whisper, more to herself than anyone else, drying her eyes before giving her mother's arm a reassuring squeeze. She looked over at Keith and Jesse. "We should get moving."

"I was just thinking," Jesse began, visibly relieved that he hadn't been the first to break their mutual silence, "We could probably push a few cars together and set up an ambush of our own for the next car that drives past."

"So we can leave other innocent people stranded just like we are now?" Riley frowned at him for even making the suggestion.

"I – I didn't mean it like that," he backpedaled, clutching for something to redeem himself with. "I just thought – maybe we could get them to slow down so we could hitch a ride."

"I doubt there would be enough room for all of us," Susan turned away from them to wipe her tears. She took a deep breath to recompose herself before facing them again, "Four hitchhikers, the original occupants, plus whatever supplies they've packed? Not likely."

"Even less of a chance they'd be willing to let us in," Keith stood from his squat beside the grave. "We don't have proper weapons to pull off an ambush, or defend ourselves if we wave down the wrong car."

"That's why I was saying we should've..." Jesse trailed off, glancing at Riley and Susan.

"I'm not looting my best friend's corpse," Keith shook his head in disdain, as useful as Nolan's taser and pepper spray might have been. He swung the shovel's blade up over his shoulder and squinted against the sun as it touched the horizon, "We better find some shelter before dark."

Riley took a moment to look around, making sure to commit her father's burial place to memory before following the others back down to the freeway, when she caught sight of something metallic gleaming through the pine trees deeper in the forest.

Watching her step as she ambled over fallen pine cones and underbrush, she drew closer to the source of the glint.

"Guys, I found something!" she called over her shoulder,

waiting for them to double back.

"What's a field fence doing out here in the middle of a forest?" Susan gazed up and down its length, hooking her finger around one of the wires and giving it a *twang*, the galvanized steel mesh faintly flashing in the sunset. "These are usually meant for keeping livestock."

Having grown up in the suburbs of Southern California, it was easy for Riley to forget that her mother had lived half her life in the rural boondocks of Nebraska.

"Probably just a wildlife barrier to keep animals off the road," Keith supposed, turning back towards the freeway.

"Well, if it's a wildlife area," Riley persisted, not ready to give up on her discovery just yet, "Maybe we can find a ranger station or a hunting cabin somewhere around here."

"Or bears," Jesse peered into the dense pine forest on the other side of the fence, "We could find bears."

"If we see any animals, it'll be a good thing," Susan took her daughter's side, "Because we'll know there's water nearby."

"And if you're wrong," Keith thrust his shovel's blade into the grass and hooked his thumbs into his belt loops, "And there's no water, no shelter, and we're wandering around in the dark, what then? If we get lost, we could be out here for days before we find our way back to the road again."

"What are we gonna do on the road anyway?" Riley placed one hand on a wooden fence post, stepped on the bottom tension wire and eased her weight up. She gritted her teeth against the dull ache in her lower back as she continued, "We could be walking for days to the next town. And we're not gonna find any water or shelter on the way there that hasn't already been taken."

"I'm sure we could find something we could use," Keith's

hesitant tone betrayed him.

"This isn't California anymore, Keith," Susan placed her hands on Riley's hips, helping her scale the fence. "We're in Wyoming now – this is the least populated state in the country. There was barely any shelter around here to begin with."

"Are we seriously leaving the road?" Jesse looked at each of them incredulously. "Did nobody hear what I said about the bears?"

"Nolan would come back to kill me if I didn't keep his girls safe," Keith sighed in resignation, tossing his shovel over and putting his boot on the fence.

Leaves and pinecones crunched underfoot as they made their way through the forest, slowly losing their visibility in the twilight. Tiny critters darted out of sight while owls beat their wings between the trees, getting ready for the night's hunt.

Riley's stomach rumbled in the silence.

They hadn't eaten anything since lunch.

"You think pine nuts come from pine trees?" Jesse wondered aloud as they came across a game trail, following Keith down the narrow dirt track.

"You'd hope so," Riley winced as she stooped to pick up a pinecone, snapping off the rigid scales as they walked. She drew a sharp breath as she splintered her thumb, and she tossed the cone off to the side.

"You're doing it wrong," Susan chided her from behind, "I'll show you how when we find a clearing."

Keith held his hand up for silence before taking a knee behind a pine.

Peering past the tree trunk, they had stumbled across more than just a clearing.

A big rundown wooden shed stood to one side of a rutted

driveway, with an old rust-bucket sedan nosing out behind the building.

"Place looks abandoned," Keith stood again, offering a nod of acknowledgment towards Riley. "At least we found our shelter for tonight."

He kept a firm grip on his shovel as they scoped out the overgrown front of the building, just in case they spooked whatever wildlife had taken up residence in and around the derelict shack.

Jesse cracked open one of the shed's double doors for Keith to venture inside, poking the shovel's blade through a pair of moldy plastic curtains as he slowly disappeared into the darkness.

The curtains swished back into place behind him, and for a moment they hung in silence, gazing at each other with weary smiles, their string of bad luck finally having turned around, when a *thwack* and a *clang* resounded from inside.

CHAPTER 21

"Keith, are you okay in there?" Susan Armstrong called, holding an armful of pinecones in the crook of her elbow.

No answer.

Riley exchanged a glance with Jesse as he stood beside the double doors.

"Dad, do you need a hand?" Jesse pulled one of the moldy plastic curtains aside and stumbled backwards in surprise, falling over his own feet.

A thin waif of a woman leapt out of the shed before anyone had time to react. Dressed in a dirty bathrobe, she planted her bare foot on Jesse's chest and leaned down low to whisper into his ear.

"It's gonna take more than a hand to get Daddy outta that shed," she snarled, bug eyes bulging and veins protruding from her forehead as she held a knife to his throat.

Riley's first thought was to make a dive for the knife, but given the ache in her lower back and the woman's blade already making an indent in Jesse's flesh, she knew that she would only be sealing his fate.

As if to solidify her decision to hold back, a pistol's barrel poked out from behind the plastic curtains, followed by the acne-scarred face of a lanky middle-aged mustached man dressed in nothing but a pair of oversized cowboy boots and a pair of undersized leopard-print panties.

"Ain't you seen the sign when you rolled in?" the leopard-print cowboy idly scratched an open sore on the side of his nose with the business end of his handgun.

"We didn't see any signs," Riley slowly held her hands up. These people were clearly deranged. She doubted that they even knew that an asteroid was heading for the West Coast, but she wasn't about to upset them any more than they already were. "We thought this place was abandoned. I'm sorry for our confusion. We'll be leaving now."

"I ain't confusin' shit!" his eyes grew wide with hot rage and he charged across the clearing towards Susan, letting off a stray bullet at the ground in the process. "Tell me what my sign says!!"

"Please believe us, we didn't see it," Susan dropped the cluster of pinecones from her arm as her feet froze in place.

"That's because it ain't there," he seized her by the upper arm and hauled her with unprecedented strength back towards the shed.

Watching her mother struggle and strain to break free of his viselike grip, Riley knew that she had to do something, but she also knew that she wouldn't be able to reason with him.

This man was beyond reason.

"Let her go!" Riley summoned her most authoritative voice – her father's police voice – staring straight into the leopard-print cowboy's unhinged eyes, "Right now, or there'll be consequences."

"Don't listen to her, Clarence!" the waiflike woman hissed

117

above Jesse's terrified face.

"Shut up, Sheila!" Clarence's lower eyelid twitched as he sized up Riley.

Riley held her ground, drilling her gaze into his, forcing out any thought of breaking eye contact from her mind, along with what he might do if she did.

"I thought I told you to get outta my house," he shoved Susan to the ground and smacked the plastic curtains aside, disappearing into the shed.

And just like that, he was gone.

"Clarence!" Sheila shrieked, still holding her knife to Jesse's throat. "You get back out here!!"

Riley helped Susan to her feet.

If they wanted to escape, this was their chance.

Jesse stared up at them in horror, too afraid to even swallow, guessing at the thoughts running through their minds. He begged them with his eyes – although whether he was begging them to help him or save themselves, Riley couldn't tell.

"You two – inside, now!" Sheila pressed her blade into Jesse's neck hard enough to draw blood to show them that she wasn't messing around. "One step outta line and I swear I'll cut your boyfriend's head off."

We're close, but we're not family, Riley pushed Susan's voice out of her head. Keith and Jesse would never leave either of them behind, not like this.

Summoning her shaky resolve, Riley clasped her mother's hand, pulled the moldy plastic curtain aside, and stepped inside the shed.

CHAPTER 22

Heart racing in her chest, Riley Armstrong blocked out the combined stench of ammonia and vinegar and nail polish remover as she stared around in the darkness of the shed, trying to make out the silhouettes looming large in every corner.

"Keith?" she asked hesitantly, dreading the answer.

"Get outta here!" his muffled voice came, followed by a pained snarl.

Just as Riley was searching for the source of his struggling, an engine from somewhere outside rumbled to life, and a glaring white light strobed into a harsh blaze overhead.

Squinting against the sudden radiance in the one-room shed, she had no choice but to let her eyes adjust slowly, taking in every shimmering detail one at a time.

Empty chip packets and crumpled beer cans littered the dirt floor. Propane tanks sat underneath a rickety folding table patched with brown chemical stains, with yellowish rubber tubes snaking up like rotten tendrils, duct taped to a pair of gas stoves.

Another set of moldy plastic curtains was draped across the opposite end of the shed, the wind from outside nudging at the flaps. Lined up along the shelves on the walls was an array of household detergents and boxes of flu medicine. A grocery basket full of small resealable plastic bags sat inside a tattered baby stroller in one corner of the room.

And in another corner was a bald fat man wearing a brown plaid shirt. His yellow teeth grinned back at Riley and Susan as he stood triumphantly over Keith – or rather, on top of him.

One shoe was planted in between Keith's shoulder blades, with the other shoe leaning on the step of the shovel, its dirt-encrusted blade resting on the side of his skull, just above the veteran policeman's ear, with dust swirling from his mouth as he heaved ragged breaths on the ground.

"Move!" Sheila hissed from behind, her thin shoulder ramming Riley and Susan deeper into the shed as she dragged Jesse inside, a small trickle of blood weeping down the front of his neck. "Get on your knees!"

With Susan squeezing her hand, Riley glanced back at Keith as they were shepherded towards the wall.

If they wanted to have any hope of saving him, they had no choice but to comply.

He was at the bald man's mercy.

One shift of the big guy's weight and Keith's skull would be cloven in two.

"Hold him there, Bobby," Sheila threw Jesse to the ground beside Riley and Susan. "Clarence! Bring me the zip ties."

"Don't you fuckin' tell me what to do," Clarence growled as he burst through the plastic curtains in the rear, hurling a handful of zip ties at her feet.

"Well? What are you waiting for?" Sheila spat, pointing her blade at their three prisoners. "Tie them up!"

"I told you, I fuckin' told you!" Clarence jammed his pistol in

Sheila's face, veins rushing his neck. "I'm gonna – I'm gonna – "

Riley looked up at the knife shaking in the woman's hand as she stared down the barrel.

She could take advantage of Sheila's distraction, lunge for her blade-hand and twist her wrist behind her back, just like her father had taught her, but with Keith's wheezing grunts in the corner, she had to think twice.

A synapse in Clarence's brain snapped as he struggled to remember what he was saying. He raked the side of his face with his grubby half-chewed fingernails, scraping off a fresh acne scab as his red-rimmed eyes wildly searched around the room.

Foaming at the mouth, he hawked up a glob of brown phlegm into a glass jar on the table beside the gas stoves.

Next, he grabbed a plastic baggie from the baby stroller, emptying its crystallized contents into the jar and swirling the filthy concoction around.

Tossing his handgun onto the table, Clarence dug around in the back of his skid-marked leopard-print panties and produced a lighter, staring intently as he burned the blackened bottom of the jar.

Bobby erupted with churlish laughter in the corner, throwing his head back and his gut forward to hold his balance, making Keith's eyes bulge underneath the amount of extra weight on the shovel's blade.

"Don't you fucking move," Sheila warned the three on their knees, stowing her knife into a pocket of her dirty bathrobe and stooping to pick up the zip ties, "Or Bobby's gonna cut himself a new hat."

Riley immediately held her hands out in feigned submission,

turning her thumbs inwards and clenching her fists as Sheila looped the cable around her wrists and yanked hard, cutting into her skin.

As tight as the restraints were, Riley knew that she could create some slack if she opened her fists and turned her palms together, but she had to wait for the right opportunity to slip her hands out.

Sheila pulled the zip ties tight around Susan and Jesse's wrists before squatting beside Keith, shoving his hands together and tying them behind his back as a sliver of spittle hung from the corner of his mouth.

"Aren't you beautiful?" Clarence's strained eyes beamed down at the bottom of his glass jar like an Old West prospector discovering flecks of gold in a pan. Plucking a grimy syringe from the dirt behind the propane tanks, he filled the tube with the liquefied crystals. Slapping his scarred forearm and smacking his lips, he stuck the needle in, "Next stop, fuckin' uhhhhh."

The physiological change was almost instant.

His pupils dilated as he straightened up with a relaxed smile, revealing a rotten set of wooden teeth.

An air of confidence exuded from the leopard-print panties-wearing cowboy as he eyed Riley, Susan and Jesse, grinding his gaunt jaws together in a storm of thought. Then, with stilted movements, he grabbed the glass jar again and walked jerkily over to Bobby.

"Spit in the jar," Clarence's eyes darted between Bobby and the three on their knees. "Spit in the jar, spit in the jar, spit in the jar."

Sheila busied herself with patting Keith's pockets while Bobby leaned over Clarence's jar.

With their captors distracted, Riley glanced up at the pistol on the folding table.

She wouldn't even have to slip out of her restraints to pick it up, aim and squeeze.

She would have to kill Bobby first, but what if he fell forward? She'd be killing Keith with the same shot.

And just like that, the moment was gone.

Clarence was emptying another baggie into the jar, and Sheila was behind the three of them, searching their pockets.

"Please, not my wedding ring," Susan begged as the woman tore it from her finger.

"You're in my house, bitch," Sheila backhanded her across the ear, sending her sideways to the ground.

"Hey!" Keith yelled, his feet kicking out and flailing into the shed's wall, shaking the shelves.

Bobby pulled the shovel up and struck him over the back of his head like a golf swing stopping short of a follow-through, the *clang* reverberating around the shed.

Riley and Jesse lurched to their feet in the same instant.

With lightning speed, Sheila kicked Jesse's legs out from underneath him, planting her bare foot on his lower back as she whipped out her knife again.

Before Riley could take two steps towards the gun on the table, Sheila grabbed a handful of her hair and wrenched her stiff neck backwards, holding the tip of the knife's blade within an inch of her eye.

"Clarence, give me a hand here!" Sheila glanced over at him as he shoved the lighter back into his panties.

"Just a minute," he had the same grimy syringe loaded up with another shot of liquefied crystals. "I just need a minute. One more minute. All I need."

123

Riley's pulse pounded in her head as she stared past Sheila's knife to see Clarence fighting an inner battle with himself, turning the needle towards his forearm again.

His lower eyelid twitched, and he snapped his attention back to their prisoners.

"Don't you see the opportunity we have here?" Clarence stared up at the ceiling while his hands drew small circles in the air, as if he was delivering an inspirational speech to a crowd with his explanatory hand gestures locked on repeat. "We can make them work for us!"

Jesse squirmed on the ground with his face in the dirt as Clarence took jarring steps towards him.

"Don't you fucking touch him!" Keith shouted, his dazed head spinning.

Bobby hit him with the shovel again, knocking him senseless this time.

With Sheila's knife still poised to take out her eye, Riley's chest heaved with shallow breaths, powerless to do anything but watch as Clarence knelt beside Jesse with the needle.

Susan propped herself up on one elbow on the ground, her eyes wide with terror.

"This'll help you relax," Clarence cooed, holding Jesse's arm steady with his pincer-like fingers. He licked the tip of the needle with his dry tongue, "There, nice and clean for you."

Jesse's pupils dilated as the drug swam through his blood-stream.

His clenched teeth parted and his struggling stopped, his entire body going limp underneath Sheila's bare foot. Only his eyes moved, darting across the floor of the shed, focusing on every detail before flicking towards the next scrap of trash.

"Now we own you," Clarence flashed his rotten wooden

teeth again before stumping over towards the baby stroller for another baggie. "Who's next?"

"Take me," Susan swallowed, looking up at Riley before summoning her resolve. "I'll do whatever you want. Just let my daughter go. Please."

"*Please*," Sheila mocked, taking her foot off Jesse's back as he began to shake. She yanked Riley backwards by the hair, still holding the blade dangerously close to her eye. "Clarence, do this one next."

"You're not injecting me with shit," Riley spat in defiance, gritting her teeth.

"I wouldn't be so sure," Bobby shouldered Sheila aside, breaking her hold on Riley's hair. He grabbed Riley's crotch with a crude grin. "You still fresh down there?"

Overcome by a claustrophobic cloud of revulsion, Riley instinctively stood on her tip toes in an effort to escape his vile touch.

Bobby let out a nauseating hum of satisfaction as he fondled the zipper of her jeans.

"You bastard!" Susan protested, struggling to get back up onto her knees.

Taking a deep breath to calm her nerves, Riley planted her feet on the ground again and stared down, past Bobby's fat sausage fingers groping her groin, locking her gaze onto his feet just like her father had taught her.

She took one step forward, bent at the knees, and launched the crown of her head up into the man's nose.

Bobby reared back with a pig's squeal, one meaty hand flying up to his blood-spattered face.

Riley spun her hands in the zip tie, creating slack in the cable, but before she could slip free, Bobby clocked her across the jaw.

Susan's screams rang hollow in Riley's ears as she staggered backwards into the shelves, knocking household chemicals to the ground as black stars of pain exploded across her retinas.

"Don't waste our product on this one," Bobby tilted his head back, pinching the bridge of his bleeding nose as he grabbed Riley by the arm. "I want her to feel *everything*."

CHAPTER 23

Riley barely felt the moldy plastic curtains streaking across her face as Bobby shoved her outside through the rear of the shed, his clammy hand crushing her upper arm.

She staggered in a stupor, still reeling from the punch to her jaw.

Her eyes swam with shadowy splotches despite the starry night painting the overgrown grass with its pale moonlight.

Susan Armstrong's screams followed them outside – begging and pleading, offering herself in Riley's place, trying to rouse Keith and Jesse, crying for Nolan to watch over their daughter.

Bobby hauled Riley past the rumbling diesel generator and a pair of broken lawn chairs towards a beaten up old caravan, covered with more patches of rust and fist-sized indents than its few remaining flecks of peeling white paint.

The door's hinges screeched open and he threw her inside, Riley's sneaker catching on the first step, sending her sprawling across the scorch-marked floor and landing in a heap on top of her tied hands.

Nobody was coming to save her now.

She knew that if she didn't fight back, she'd die – or worse, she'd wish she did.

The bald fat man picked her up again and tossed her onto a musty stained mattress.

Still in a daze, Riley's head lolled from side to side as she scanned the shadowy caravan for something to hit him with, only to see countless dead matches and a cockroach crawling into an empty beer can.

"You fucked up my nose, you stupid bitch," his voice had a nasally pitch as blood leaked from his pig snout. He began undoing the buttons of his brown plaid shirt, his hairy gut spilling out, glistening with a sheen of sweat. "Now I'm gonna make *you* bleed."

Riley aimed a clumsy kick at one of his kneecaps, but he caught her foot and twisted her ankle until her aching lower back screamed at her to roll over.

The whole caravan rocked as Bobby's knees fell on either side of her pelvis, pinning her down with his weight.

She was in the worst possible position now, her face pressed against the yellowed moth-eaten mattress with her bound hands caught underneath her stomach.

Heart hammering in her chest, she struggled with the zip tie around her wrists, straining desperately to slip her hands free.

The sound of his trousers rustling down spiked her adrenaline, the icy surge tearing her out of her dazed stupor, and in a final last-ditch effort, she managed to wrench one of her hands out from underneath her torso.

"What the fu–" was all Bobby managed to blurt out before she blindly reached back and crushed whatever tiny package he was carrying.

She dug her fingernails in and *twisted* as he screamed in whistling silence, the excruciating pain escalating beyond the range of his vocal chords.

He careened to one side, freeing her as he fell back against the wall of the caravan, feebly trying to swat away her hand, every jolting impact an agonizing reminder that she had him by the balls.

Riley reared up on her knees, savoring the anguish scrawled across his face for one fleeting moment before pulling her hand free of his crotch and ramming the crook of her thumb straight up into his throat, crushing his voice box.

She drew back to strike him again, but something inside his throat had ruptured, and he made a guttural gurgling sound, as if he was about to retch. Blood seeped from the corner of his mouth as the veins in his forehead bulged, his eyebrows arching in confusion.

Bobby's fat sausage fingers floated up from his ruined crotch, one hand gingerly touching his throat while the other slowly reached up towards Riley, wordlessly begging for help as his eyes swam with tears.

She jerked away from the would-be rapist, watching with grim satisfaction as his face turned blue.

CHAPTER 24

Riley Armstrong stared down at Bobby's corpse, his lifeless gaze etching itself into her retinas. Her hands trembled as she tossed the zip tie at him, the adrenaline dissipating from her shaky fingers.

And then the realization came – she had just killed a man.

She didn't regret it for one second, and she would have gladly done it again.

But until this very moment, she hadn't stopped to think about just how much her entire world had been turned upside down since yesterday morning, and the extent of what she was willing to do to keep whatever was left of her warped world turning.

She couldn't afford to dwell on it for too long though.

Her fight wasn't done yet.

Her mother, Keith and Jesse were still stuck inside the shed with the other two psychopaths.

Riley searched around the caravan for a weapon, pulling open stubborn drawers and creaking cupboards, only to find a box of bullets and half a can of baked beans crawling with more maggots than beans.

Another scream from the shed cut her search short.

Riley stepped out of the caravan empty-handed.

She padded over the path of bent grass, past the rumbling diesel generator and the broken lawn chairs, creeping towards the rear entrance of the shed.

Ducking down beside the pair of moldy plastic curtains, she pulled the bottom portion aside, just slightly, as if the wind had nudged the flap open.

"... Bobby's done, I'll head out back," Clarence was burning the bottom of the glass jar with his lighter again, absentmindedly going over his plans for the evening, "Have my turn, then Bobby, then me again. Just like we done Sheila."

Gazing through the thin gap between the curtains, Riley could see Jesse rolling around on the ground, empty chip packets crinkling underneath him as he tried to make sense of the poisons polluting his body.

"Wake up, Keith," Susan whimpered as Jesse spontaneously kicked out at her thigh.

"They're gonna find somewhere else to sleep," Sheila spat, pacing circles around Susan, Keith and Jesse as she contemplated their new companions. "I'm not sharing my mattress with these filthy fuckers as well."

Riley caught the gleam of the pistol resting on the rickety folding table beside the pair of gas stoves.

Clarence was still too close to the table though, and Sheila and Jesse were wildcards. Either one of them could get in her way at any time, and she only had one chance at grabbing the gun.

A low groan sounded from the far corner of the shed as Keith shook his head.

He blinked hard at the ground as he began to come to his senses again.

"Looks like we got our next customer," Sheila pulled the folds of her dirty bathrobe apart, revealing her hairy legs as she squatted over the top of Keith, tracing her knife's edge up the curve of his spine.

"I'm gonna do the woman first," Clarence pulled his grimy syringe out of the jar, filled with another load of liquefied crystals. "She's cryin' too much. She ain't gonna be cryin' in a minute. Why do they always cry?"

Clarence was halfway across the shed when he paused to ponder the thought, scratching at the bony ribs underneath his armpit with his grubby half-chewed fingernails, digging a set of angry red grooves into his sallow skin.

"Go ahead," Sheila drew her blade underneath Keith's throat, threatening to slash it open if he moved, "This one's not going anywhere."

"Jesse?" Keith caught his son writhing on the ground in the corner of his eye, "What the fuck did you do to my boy!?"

Riley had to make a choice – her mother or Keith.

If she ran in now, Sheila would cut his throat without hesitation.

But if Riley waited too long for an opportunity that might not even present itself, Clarence would pump a shot of hard drugs into Susan, doing irreversible damage to her body, not to mention the number of infectious diseases in the grimy syringe itself.

Icy adrenaline pulsing through her veins, Riley tore the moldy plastic curtains apart and charged into the shed.

With all her weight, she shoved Clarence sideways over Jesse's flailing body, sending the leopard-print cowboy to the ground as he thrust the needle up into the air to keep it from breaking.

Carried by her momentum, Riley slammed her hip into the rickety folding table, the whole bench collapsing.

Her hand shot out to snatch up the pistol by its barrel before everything fell, the yellowish rubber tubes snapping free from the propane tanks as the pair of gas stoves crashed to the floor.

"Riley?" Susan asked in disbelief, a glad smile shining through her tears.

"You stupid whore!" Sheila shrieked, poising to open Keith's throat as his bound hands struggled in vain behind his back. "Say goodbye to everyone you love!"

"Back at you, bitch!" Riley screamed, swinging the pistol up.

Riley had never fired a gun.

She had no idea how to aim.

Across the length of the shed, Sheila may as well have been squatting down by the freeway.

Clarence was closer, but Riley doubted that Sheila would even care whether he lived or died. On top of everything else, she had no idea whether the loose propane connections would cause the tanks to explode if she pulled the trigger.

But none of that mattered.

"I'm sorry!" Sheila dropped the knife and slowly held her hands up, her eyes wide with terror. "I barely even touched him, look!"

Keith rolled away unscathed, the flesh of his neck still intact.

Riley's pulse pounded in her head, the pistol rattling in her shaky hands as she held it steady on the one thing that Sheila cared about – her next fix, the gun's barrel trained on the grocery basket full of plastic baggies in the tattered baby stroller.

"We can make more, woman!" rigid cords in Clarence's neck flexed as he took a wide swing at Keith with the syringe, narrowly missing his shoulder.

Susan lunged at the acne-scarred man on the ground, her bound hands wrestling with his wrist as he turned the needle on her instead.

Keith stomped his police boots into Clarence's face while Susan rammed her knees up into his spine, the three of them engaged in a savage scuffle as they kicked up dirt and debris across the shed.

Riley kept her eyes locked on Sheila as she wheeled the tattered baby stroller around the wreckage of the folding table, still holding the pile of plastic baggies at gunpoint.

She stopped short of the waiflike woman – close enough to aim at her now – and upended the contents of the grocery basket on the ground.

"Eat it," Riley ordered, turning the gun on Sheila, "All of it."

"Really?" Sheila's eyes lit up with glee, her gaze darting from Riley to the pile of drugs scattered across the dirt. She glanced at Clarence as he struggled to fend off both Susan and Keith. "They never let me touch the baby."

Free to eat the forbidden fruit, Sheila seized the closest baggie, ripped it open and dumped the crystallized chemicals into her mouth. Her raspy brown tongue licked the insides of the plastic bag before starting on the next one.

Riley would have pitied Sheila – slave to a drug that she probably never even wanted – but whatever humanity was once within the waiflike woman had been scorched out of her a long time ago.

"Susan!?" Keith's shout ripped Riley's attention away from Sheila.

Her mother was on top of Clarence now, his thumbs digging into her sides as she held the syringe aloft in her bound hands.

Screaming in agony, she brought the needle down into one of his wild eyes, pumping the poison into the bloody mess of his retina.

He showed no reaction, his brain's pain receptors completely inert.

With her midsection still caught in his grip, Susan Armstrong balled her fists into a wrecking ball and rammed the syringe home.

"Riley?" she wheezed as she extracted herself from Clarence's spasming hands, glancing around the shed with a crazed and breathless smile. "Are you okay?"

CHAPTER 25

"He's burning up," Keith Bowman knelt by Jesse's side, checking his pulse. "Go check if they've got any water."

"I already looked twice," Riley held up the box of bullets from the caravan out back. "This is all I could find."

"How the fuck did these people live out here?" he shot an angry glare at Sheila.

The drug addict was convulsing in the corner of the shed, frothing at the mouth with an empty plastic baggie caught in between her rotten teeth.

Repulsed, but without a shred of sympathy, Riley collected their stolen belongings from Sheila while the waiflike woman's eyes rolled up into the back of her head.

Susan breathed easy again the moment she was reunited with her wedding ring.

"We should get outta here," Susan glanced pointedly at the propane tanks, their connections knocked loose by the collapsed table. "Maybe we can find some water along the way."

"Did you find any keys, at least?" Keith's whiskey-cured voice strained as he picked up his son.

Jesse's arm dangled to the ground as he stared up at the

ceiling of the shed, his eyes zipping rapidly around the rafters, as if he was experiencing a waking dream – even as Keith carried him through the plastic curtains and out of the living nightmare.

"Yeah, I found some," Riley patted her pocket.

Relief washed across Keith and Susan's faces as they heard the faint metallic jingle in her jeans.

Bobby's face had looked quite different.

Outside, the night sky was clear, filled with stars as a full moon shone down, lighting their way around the side of the shed towards the old rust-bucket sedan.

Riley always seemed to forget just how many stars were visible in the sky whenever they were on their way to Grandma Eleanor's farm in Nebraska. Back in Redhurst, the far-flung tapestry of twinkling torches was almost invisible behind the thick veil of smog and light pollution that hung over the city.

But as serene and tranquil as the moment was, the thought that an asteroid was currently hurtling towards them from somewhere within that same vast expanse was enough to bring Riley's feet back to the ground.

"I'll drive," Susan volunteered as she walked around the side of the sedan. She massaged the red rings around her wrists before holding up her hand.

"Shotgun," Riley tossed the keys over the roof of the car and pulled the passenger door open with a creak.

There was no argument from Keith as he laid Jesse down in the backseat, silently cradling his son's head in his lap.

The old rust-bucket's interior came exactly as advertised.

The cracked brown leather of the seat upholstery was mostly held together with duct tape. A makeshift ashtray had been melted into the surface of the dashboard. The driver's headrest spun around on one support column as Susan ducked inside.

"This thing is a death trap," Riley reached up over her shoulder for her seatbelt, giving it a small tug, only for the strap's bracket to snap off the center column.

"As long as it runs, that's all that matters," Susan said as she turned the ignition, the engine grating and wheezing unconvincingly before rumbling to life.

They all ducked down in their seats as a loud *crack* sounded from outside, and Riley swung Clarence's pistol back towards the shed.

Hunching over the steering wheel, Susan shifted the car into gear, flicked the headlights on and gunned the engine down the rutted driveway, refusing to sit completely upright in her seat until they were bordered on both sides by the gloomy pine forest.

"You should probably have this," Riley checked the pistol's safety lever underneath the moonlight and looked back over her shoulder, wincing as her stiff neck returned.

"Hold onto it for a while," Keith swayed from side to side in the backseat as they hit a rough patch in the dirt road. He glanced down at his son, "I've seen too many guys lash out when they're tweaking. Best keep it up front."

Riley stashed Clarence's gun and the extra bullets into the glove box. The compartment was overflowing with empty candy wrappers, but it was cleaner than the rest of the car – comparatively, at least.

They ducked again as another *crack* rang through the trees somewhere behind them.

"It's probably just the engine," Jesse croaked from the backseat.

Keith breathed a sigh of relief, although his respite was short-lived, turning into a strained grunt as he fought to keep his son from sitting up.

"Too much fuel, not enough air," Jesse spewed mechanical jargon from his father's lap, "Too much air, not enough fuel. The exhaust's leaking, the air filter's dirty, the fuel injectors are faulty, the spark plugs – the spark plugs – the spark plugs. It's probably just the engine."

"Jesse, do me a favor, just breathe," Keith laid the back of his hand against Jesse's forehead. "Fuck. This car got air-con?"

"You're in luck," Susan replied in a taut voice as she looked up at the rearview mirror and sidelong at Riley.

Catching her mother's glance, Riley leaned over the center console, toggling the old dials on the climate control until cool air flowed. It wasn't exactly warm in the state of Wyoming, but it was the best that they could do for Jesse.

Supposing that if the air-conditioning was still working in the decrepit old sedan, Riley tried the radio next, flipping through channels of static for any news reports.

"Try the AM stations," Susan suggested as they emerged from the backwoods, the car's tires finding purchase on a gravel road snaking through an overgrown field.

Riley switched the bandwidth and managed to pick up tinny voices that faded in and out. Straining her ears, she listened for any mention of the chaos in California, or anywhere along the West Coast.

"Nothing," she furrowed her eyebrows in disbelief, flipping to another station. "No riots in the cities, no carjacks on the freeways, no asteroids. They're just talking about the weather and sports as if everything's normal."

"Probably the same reason they were keeping it quiet back in Cali," Keith supposed, despite having also attempted to maintain his silence for their advantage. "They don't want our panic spreading across the rest of the country."

"What about word of mouth?" Riley tried a third station. "Something must have been posted on the internet by now. They can't keep this quiet forever."

"When's the last time either of you had any internet?" Susan gazed intently at the road ahead.

"I doubt we're gonna get anything out here," Riley checked her phone all the same, its once-familiar screen almost foreign to her after everything else that she had witnessed. It was still out of service. "See? We're in the middle of nowhere."

"That's the thing about civilization," Keith sucked his front teeth, staring out the window at the stars in the sky, "When it all falls apart, everywhere is the middle of nowhere."

CHAPTER 26

"Hey, check it out," Riley sat up in the passenger seat and pointed out the windshield, "There's a gas station up ahead."

They were heading east again, but they weren't back on the freeway just yet.

Maybe that was why the lonely Pump and Go gas station had been spared the worst of the mass exodus from the coast.

Huddled opposite the shadowy entrance of an immense lot filled with hulking farm machinery, the gas station was the only place with its doors still open for business this late at night for miles around.

"Slow down," Keith leaned sideways in the backseat to see clearer through the windshield, scanning either side of the empty highway as they approached the entrance. "Look out for anything suspicious. We might be driving into another trap."

"I doubt it," Susan pulled in and steered towards the pumps. "Any thieves around here would already have their hands full turning this place over."

"Yeah, I don't think thieves put things *onto* the shelves," Riley peered at the sole store attendant restocking the aisles.

"Alright, I'm gonna stay in here with Jesse," Keith settled

back into his seat, still keeping a wary eye on their surroundings. "Riley, go grab whatever you can. He needs water, and I think we could all use some food."

"Well, I was planning on staying hungry, but if you insist," she sassed him as she creaked her door open, sharing a smirk with her mother, "It's a good thing we brought you along, Keith. You're a real benefit to have."

"Fuck outta here," he chuckled before holding his hands up, eyes wide, "Sorry, Susan."

Riley climbed out of the car, smiling to herself as her mother gave him an unimpressed hum. She walked across the concrete lot towards the store, shaking her head as she pondered the absurdity of still being able to crack jokes even after everything they had seen and been through since leaving Redhurst.

Approaching the sliding glass doors, she caught her reflection, and for a fleeting moment, she glimpsed Nolan Armstrong grinning beside her, but when she turned, he was gone, along with her smile.

Riley navigated through the store's aisles lined with chocolate bars, sour sweets and sodium-laced packets of chips. The gas station wasn't exactly a hub for health food, but the way her stomach was rumbling, she would have settled for a bag of deep-fried salt.

Surprisingly though, she managed to stack up a decent haul on the counter, picking up packets of trail mixes, boxes of muesli bars, along with some strips of string cheese and beef jerky. Naturally, there were more bottles of soda and energy drinks than good old-fashioned water in the fridge cases, but she grabbed as much water as she could carry.

The store attendant muttered under his breath while ringing up her total, making mental notes of which items he would have to restock later, in between stealing obvious glances at her.

"I haven't seen you arou–"

"I'll pay for the gas too," Riley cut across his attempt to hit on her. After leaving three corpses to rot out in the Wyoming wilderness, she wasn't particularly in the mood for letting anybody shoot their shot with her. "Do you take card?"

"Cash only, sweetheart," he finished bagging up the groceries.

Sweetheart? Riley raised an eyebrow at him, biting her tongue.

She didn't have any cash on her, but her mother or Keith might.

Or, she could grab Clarence's gun out of the glove box and see how much of a "sweetheart" he thought she was then.

What difference would it make if she actually paid for the groceries anyway?

It was only a matter of time before somebody else came and robbed the gas station – it might as well have been them.

No, we're not that far gone, she thought to herself.

She wasn't ready to prey on the innocent.

Not yet.

"Hey, that looks like Bobby's car," the store attendant glanced outside at the old rust-bucket sedan as Susan hung the fuel hose back on the pump. "You must be Sheila, right?"

"Y-yeah, that's me," Riley's pitch changed as she rubbed the back of her neck. "How did you know?"

"He talks about you a lot," the cashier leaned over the counter, shamelessly sizing her up. "He said you were hot, but I didn't think he was actually telling the truth! He's still coming in tomorrow, right?"

"I'm not sure," she bit her bottom lip, wondering whether

the attendant was expecting a social call or a drug delivery. "I don't think so. He said he's got a sore throat, so he just sent us to pick up a few things."

"Typical fucking Bobby," he shook his head with a sigh. "Ah well, more hours, more money for me, right?"

"Yeah, crazy," Riley retreated a step from the counter, her pulse pounding. She glanced outside as her mother climbed back into the sedan. She didn't care about the groceries anymore. She just wanted to leave. "Speaking of money, I think we've got some in the car."

"Oh, don't worry about it," the store attendant printed the receipt, scribbled a note on the back and threw it into the cash register. "Whatever we buy just comes straight outta our pay checks. Easier that way. Didn't Bobby tell you?"

Riley breathed a small sigh of relief as he pushed the bags of groceries towards her.

Just as she was hooking her hands through the plastic loops, a thought crossed his face. He glanced down at the groceries, looked up at Riley, and then peered outside.

"You said Bobby sent you?" his hand crept underneath the counter, his lustful stare now laced with suspicion. "He's got a nut allergy."

The trail mix, she swallowed, her pupils dilating at the packets poking out of the bags.

She couldn't believe their luck.

Riley supposed that the drug addicts had to get their supplies from somewhere, but the fact that Bobby worked *here* with a colleague who knew just enough about his pitiful life to catch her out – what were the chances?

"Those are for me," she looked up from the trail mixes, brushing stray strands of hair over her ear. "I'm sick of eating bags of chips all the time. I need some variety."

"Doesn't explain why you just offered to pay," his hand was still underneath the counter.

"Yeah, typical fucking Bobby, right?" Riley folded her arms, doubling down even as her heart thumped in her chest. "Of course he wasn't gonna tell me that all this could come straight outta his pay check. Selfish prick. You know what?" she grabbed a handful of chocolate bars from a display and threw them into one of the bags. "Add that to whatever he owes. Next time, he can pick up his own shit. I don't care how sick he is."

With a scowl, she snatched the grocery bags off the counter, spun on her heel and marched towards the sliding glass doors.

It took all of her willpower not to break out into a headlong run towards the car.

Without looking back, she shimmied between the gas pumps, cracked the passenger door open and threw the bags down onto the gritty floor mat.

"Don't you wanna put them in the trunk?" Susan gazed at her curiously.

"Just drive," Riley breathed, glancing at the store attendant staring back at them through the window. "Those drug addicts had friends."

CHAPTER 27

Riley struck out with the heel of her palm, missing her menace's throat, smashing her hand into something solid instead.

A flash of glaring white light blinded her retinas, and she threw up her arm to shield her eyes.

"Morning," Keith Bowman chuckled behind her. "Have a good sleep?"

She sat up and stretched in the passenger seat of the decrepit old sedan, blinking groggily at the dent on the dashboard.

"What time is it?" she massaged her wrist and looked around. "Where's Mom?"

They were parked on the side of a dirt road in the middle of an overgrown field. At the foot of a slope in the distance was a wooden fence with a flock of sheep grazing farther up the hill.

"She just stepped out to chuck everything into the trunk," he looked down at Jesse still lying in his lap, "Can't tell you the time though. Phone's dead."

Riley rolled her neck from side to side, the stiffness from yesterday's crash on the freeway having cleared up. Her lower back was still painful though, and another night spent sleeping in a car seat hadn't done her any favors.

Framed by the backdrop of the open trunk's rusty lid, Keith was no longer wearing the makeshift bandage across the gash on his forehead, a thin scab having formed just above his eyebrow. Even without his police uniform, kit belt and sidearm, he still had the same stony gaze of a man ready to spring into action at the slightest sign of trouble.

Jesse was lying across the backseat with his eyes closed, twitching with fits and starts, probably reliving the same nightmare that Riley had just woken up from. His face was covered in a sheen of sweat, as if he had been running a marathon.

"How's he doing?" she asked as Susan shut the trunk.

"He dropped off to sleep as soon as the sun came up," Keith rubbed at his own eyes, bloodshot and weary. "I think he's through the worst of it. Just sweating it outta his system now."

"Were you up all night?" Riley winced at the pain in her lower back as she reached across the center console to open up the driver's side door, her mother's hands full.

"Had to be," he shrugged, nodding down at Jesse.

"Good morning," Susan chirped as she sat behind the steering wheel, the old rust-bucket sedan creaking as she handed them muesli bars and strips of string cheese.

"We couldn't have stopped in at a motel?" Riley lifted her back off the seat with a grimace before peeling a packet of cheese open.

"Had that conversation," Susan glanced up at the rearview mirror.

"Wanted to stay off the main roads," Keith explained around a mouthful of muesli, "We're driving a stolen car, remember?"

"Half the cars heading east by now are probably stolen," Riley bit off a chunk of cheese, not in the mood to strip each string

147

one by one.

"Yeah, this one sticks out like a whore at a wedding though," he laughed before plucking crumbs from Jesse's face. "Sorry, I shouldn't be talking about Karen."

Riley snorted and glanced sidelong at her mother, expecting her to reprimand him, but even Susan failed to stifle her smirk.

"But even if we don't get pulled over," he took another mouthful of the muesli bar, "There are still people out there who want the gas in our tank, and whatever else we've got."

"We should be in Nebraska by now," Susan guessed by the look of the countryside. "Surely all that chaos is behind us, right?"

"Maybe," he shrugged, looking them both in the eye before staring out the window. "All I know is, I've never had this many near-death experiences in the same week, even with all my years on the force, and it's only been a couple days."

They chewed in silence for a while, only disturbed by the sound of their plastic wrappers crinkling.

"Could you teach me how to shoot?" Riley glanced at her mother before gazing back at Keith.

"Didn't Nolan?" Keith's eyes shifted between them both.

"I – I didn't think it was necessary," Susan looked down at her lap for a moment. Taking a breath, she sat up in her seat again, "Gun safety, yes. Absolutely. But not how to shoot."

"I can give her some pointers," he offered before matching Riley's gaze. "You're not gonna be a professional with just one lesson, but it'll be a start."

That's all Riley wanted.

She knew how to hold her own in a physical struggle, but hand-to-hand techniques only went so far.

In a world where people were willing to take whatever they

wanted from everyone else, she had to learn how to defend herself by any means necessary.

Susan agreed that it was time for her daughter to learn, but she chose to stay in the car with Jesse in case he woke up.

"Alright, tell me what you know before we start," Keith led Riley towards the wooden fence at the bottom of the hill where the flock of sheep were grazing.

"Only point the barrel at things you wanna kill," Riley recited her father's safety lessons, holding Clarence's pistol at the ground. "Never assume the gun's empty. Squeeze, don't pull."

"Squeeze, don't pull," he echoed with an amused smile. "You know what that means?"

"Not really," she admitted, not even sure where she had heard it from.

"Thought so," Keith held his hand out. "Let me see that for a second."

Riley almost passed it to him, when she paused, taking a moment to check the safety lever first.

Keith hummed his approval as he examined the gun, before ejecting the magazine and cocking back the slide to clear the chamber.

"Gonna start you off dry," he knelt to pick up the discarded bullet before handing the pistol back to her. "Second rule after safety is your grip. Two hands. Hold it firm. Limp wrists get your gun jammed. Put your thumb below the slide."

He paused his rapid-fire instructions until she found a grip that she was comfortable with, cupping the bottom of her right hand and the pistol's hilt with her left.

"Take your finger off the trigger," he started again, "You don't even know what you're aiming at. Don't touch it until you've got your target in your sights."

Riley laid her forefinger alongside the trigger guard, flashing back to when her mother had blasted a hole into the dashboard of their red suburban.

"Don't tell me we're shooting at the sheep," she furrowed her eyebrows at Keith.

"Depends on your aim," he chuckled with a glance at the top of the hill. "I just want you to hit that fence post."

Riley adopted a fighter's stance, turning at the torso with her left foot forward and right foot back. She brought the gun up, closed one eye and squeezed the stiff trigger impotently.

"Alright, ram this up its ass and let's see what you got," Keith handed her the magazine. "Make sure you line up those sights before you touch the trigger."

Riley slammed the magazine up into the hilt, thumbed the slide release, and flipped off the safety lever.

Her hands were shaking.

She'd had no problem holding the pistol last night in the drug lab, but that was only because of all the adrenaline coursing through her veins.

Now, she was about to squeeze off a shot straight after breakfast.

"Breathe," Keith murmured in her ear. "It's just a fence post. Who gives a fuck?"

CRACK!

The gun barked in her hands, sending a shockwave up her arms as the report smacked her eardrums.

The flock of sheep gave up a faint bleat and disappeared over the hill.

"Did I hit it?" she peered at the fence post, a high pitch ringing in her ears.

"You hit something," he tried to sound encouraging. "This

time, I want you to press the trigger *slow* until it breaks."

Squeeze, don't pull, she lined up her sights again, applying small increments of pressure on the trigger.

CRACK!

A chip of wood splintered off the top corner of the fence post. The sound wasn't as loud this time.

Or maybe she had already blown her eardrums.

"You shoot like your dad," Keith eyed the target.

"Really?" she lowered the pistol to the ground.

"Wasn't meant to be a compliment," he chuckled before a sigh robbed him of his grin. "Come on, let's get outta here before Old MacDonald shows up with a rifle."

"That's it?" she flipped the safety lever on.

"We don't have enough ammo to practice properly," he turned to walk back towards the car. "If we run into any trouble down the road, don't be a hero trying to join the shootout. Keep your gun down, wait until they're close enough, and then put a bullet in them at point blank range."

"How many people have you shot?" Riley glanced sidelong at him as they walked back down the dirt road.

"I've got plenty numbers I can brag about," he sucked his front teeth and looked up at the scattered clouds in the sky. "But that's not one of them."

"It's just," her sneakers ground to a halt as she searched for the right words, "What if we have to kill someone else on our way to the farm?"

"Those three from last night still on your mind?" Keith stopped and studied her.

Riley nodded.

"Get used to it," he held up a hand at Susan as she watched them from the car. "Every time you take a life, they don't just fuck off into the sunset. They latch on to you, and you gotta carry them with you wherever you go."

"They don't fade away?" in the back of Riley's mind, she could still see Bobby screaming in whistling silence, wordlessly begging for help as blood seeped from the corner of his mouth.

"The bad ones do," Keith admitted, nodding in silence for a moment. He took a deep breath. "Your dad probably never even told you. Six years ago, we responded to a call out for a neighborhood disturbance. Some kid got into his parents' gun collection and started threatening the neighbors."

"How old was he?" Riley clapped a hand over her mouth.

"He went to juvie, that's all I know," Keith shrugged, blinking up at the sky. "We got him to drop the rifle. Your dad cuffed him, led him back to the car. I caught movement in one of the upstairs windows though. Nolan didn't see it, but I swear there was a gun pointed at his back. I didn't think twice – I pulled my sidearm and I took the shot."

"You saved my dad's life," Riley furrowed her eyebrows, cocking her head slightly at the remorse creasing his face.

"Except I didn't," Keith choked, rubbing at his bloodshot eyes. "It was that dumbass fucking kid's five-year-old brother holding a toy airplane. He was dead before we even got upstairs. I can still see the shock on his face, clear as I'm seeing you right now."

He glanced at the old rust-bucket sedan, and then at the wooden fence, as if he was making sure nobody else was listening.

"All the bad ones I've killed," he took a few steps back towards the hill, raised his hand and pointed. "They're all on the other side of that fence. But if I look straight at them, they disappear. That one kid though. He's right in front of me.

He – he never leaves. He's still staring at me with his monkey pajamas and his stupid fucking airplane."

Riley glanced at her mother sitting behind the steering wheel, not knowing what to say.

"Whatever you do," Keith swallowed as they resumed their slow walk back towards the car. "You wanna keep as many bodies on the other side of that fence as possible. Think real hard before you pull the trigger, because the ones on this side of the fence fuck you for life."

CHAPTER 28

"I think I know that town," Susan Armstrong murmured through the chainsaw whirrs of Keith's snoring as she peered over the steering wheel. "That's Clementine."

Riley sat up in the scratchy passenger seat as the distant dots of a small town grew in the distance.

"How far are we to Grandma's?" she didn't have the vaguest idea of her way around Nebraska, but she looked around for a familiar landmark anyway, seeing nothing but rolling prairies and far-off forests.

"I'd say just over an hour," Susan's relief was written across her face, glad to be back on familiar turf again after wending their way through the backcountry. "It's a straight shot from here though, not long now."

"I can't wait that long," Jesse piped up from the backseat, still lying down in his father's lap, staring blankly at the back of the driver's seat. "I'm starving."

"We've got some food in the trunk," Riley offered, glancing sidelong at her mother. "Maybe we can pull over when we get clear of this town?"

"No, you don't understand," he sat up, sweat glistening

across his face. "I need to eat *real food*, right now!"

Keith's snores died and he shook awake with a start.

"What's going on?" he snapped himself upright and stared around the car. "Jesse? How are you feeling?"

"I'm dying of hunger and thirst," Jesse swayed in his seat, pressing his hands into his temples. "And they don't even care!"

"Hold on," Keith reached down for the bottle of water between his boots, "We've got some beef jerky in the –"

"I don't want that!" Jesse smacked the water bottle out of his father's hands. He opened up the door on the passenger side while they were still speeding down the highway. "None of you are listening!"

"Shut the door!" Susan swerved to the side just as an old farm truck roared past, blaring its horn at them.

"Jesse, pull yourself together!" Riley turned in her seat as Susan wrestled with the steering wheel, the decrepit old sedan fishtailing to a lurching stop on the side of the road.

"I've got him," Keith caught hold of Jesse's wrists and twisted his hands behind his back. "Riley, can you get the water?"

She checked the side mirror for any other approaching vehicles before climbing out of the car.

Jesse was thrashing around in the backseat despite his father's hold on him.

Riley's hand darted in between his wild kicks and knee thrusts, snatching the water bottle up off the floor.

"This car doesn't have seatbelts," she snapped at Jesse as she unscrewed the lid, squirting water into his face. "You could've gotten us all killed, you idiot!"

"I'm sorry," his kicking stopped, the splash of water like a

155

cold shock to his polluted system. He heaved shallow breaths as he came back to his senses. "I'm just – it's –"

He leaned towards Riley, his tearful eyes on the water bottle.

Keith gave her a small nod, and she reluctantly brought the bottle's rim to Jesse's lips.

"Let's head into town," Keith suggested, watching his son gulp greedily as water spilled down his shirt.

"What if it isn't safe?" Riley turned to look through the windshield, scanning for any signs of trouble in the distance.

"If it's bad, we'll keep going," Keith was still holding his son's hands behind his back, even as Jesse spluttered and choked on the water. "But we need to find him a doctor."

"I'll take us to the diner," Susan nodded, gesturing for Riley to get back in her seat. "Jesse's right, he needs some real food after what he's been through. I think we all do. We can find a doctor after."

Their old rust-bucket sedan was right at home with the rest of the local traffic along the wide avenue of Main Street.

Some of the vehicles looked like third-generation family heirlooms. Station wagons that had soldiered on past their mid-life crisis were parked in front of brick-lined banks and single-story offices. Mud-bellied pickup trucks sat outside hunting stores and tackle shops.

The town's inhabitants were going about their daily business, a trio of mothers pushing strollers across the middle of the quiet street, neighbors stopping for brief chats with each other on the sidewalks, while the local real estate agent locked up his office for lunch.

Whatever tension the travel-worn transients had felt in the sedan was quickly waning away with each smiling face they glimpsed.

The insanity that had spread from the coast hadn't yet taken up residence in this peaceful town.

Susan parked a few doors down from the diner.

Across the street, in front of the general store, a man wearing a Hawaiian shirt was hastily lining bags of groceries around stacks of suitcases in the back of his dust-covered minivan while his wife kept an eye on their kids, clutching them close every time someone passed by.

Guess this place isn't completely panic-free, Riley supposed, although one exception wasn't the end of the world.

If anything, she was grateful for the reality check.

With one foot on the pavement, she pulled Clarence's pistol out of the glove box and checked the safety lever before sliding it into the waistband of her jeans at the small of her back.

Susan noticed, pursing her lips in disapproval, but she said nothing.

The small bell above the diner's entrance chimed as they pushed the door open, and a few of the townsfolk glanced in their direction.

A woman garbed in camouflage hunting gear paused with a pint of beer halfway up to her lips. Sandwich flecks flew from a mechanic's mouth as he wolf-whistled at Riley and Susan, although he averted his gaze at the sight of Keith bringing up the rear.

Booth by booth, the locals whispered and turned around, shooting curious stares in their direction.

Riley supposed that they didn't get many out-of-towners dropping in for lunch, but then she realized what they were looking at.

Keith had a fresh scab just above his eyebrow, Jesse's face was covered with a sheen of sweat while his shirt was still wet with water, and the amount of grime on Riley and Susan couldn't have looked much better.

Riley found herself wanting a shower and a change of clothes, or at the very least, something to tie up her greasy hair with.

"What can we do for y'all?" a portly man nudged a waitress aside behind the counter, wearing a guarded expression and a shirt with *Herb* stitched above his breast pocket.

"We're just here for lunch," Riley answered quickly, putting on a smile to dissuade any hostilities, the gawking townsfolk soon turning back to their meals.

"That's it?" Herb eyed them suspiciously before relenting, not wanting to turn away new customers. He grunted, "Table in the corner then."

They shuffled into the corner booth, salivating as they scanned the menus and made their orders with one of the waitresses.

A news reporter's voice droned on from the TV suspended above the counter as the chatter and clatter of cutlery resumed.

The bell above the entrance chimed again, with the man in the Hawaiian shirt holding the door open for his family to shuffle in, quickly settling into a booth and glancing around.

"And now for the asteroid rumored to be heading for the West Coast," the news broadcast cut through the noise of the diner.

"Finally," Riley breathed, perking up in her seat, the pistol in her waist rubbing against her lower back. "Could you turn that up?"

Herb sighed, reluctantly increasing the volume and crossing his hairy arms as the other patrons tuned in.

"There is absolutely no reason to panic," the anchorman beamed at the camera. "Astronomers predict that it won't even enter our atmosphere. Life will go on as normal." He turned to his co-host with a grin. "And we can all be happy that our insurance premiums won't be rising this year. And now for the weather..."

"I knew my sister was overreacting!" the mechanic called out across the diner.

"Gonna take a hell of a lot more than a rock to send us packing," the hunter declared, setting her beer down on the counter. "This is America, motherfucker. If that asteroid comes anywhere near us, we'd nuke the son of a bitch back out to space!"

"So everything that's happened over the past few days," Riley dropped her eyes to the table in disbelief as a waitress brought their plates over. "It was all for nothing?"

"Nolan..." the color drained from Susan's drawn face as she continued to stare up at the TV, certain that she had misheard the broadcast.

"Here's your food, Jesse," Keith sucked his front teeth and gazed out the window at the overcast sky, shaking his head in silence.

"Are you guys hearing yourselves?" Jesse picked up his knife and fork, frowning at them all as the waitress set down his plate. "When the people in charge of pushing fear as a commodity say *don't panic* – it's time to fucking panic."

He tucked into his scrambled eggs and baked beans like a ravenous wolf, barely pausing to chew.

Having overheard their conversation, a man in the next booth folded up his newspaper and stood to throw a fistful of change onto the table before heading for the exit.

"Look, Daddy!" a little girl stood up on the bench, ignoring her milkshake and pointing out the window as she gazed back at the man in the Hawaiian shirt, "The people from the freeway are here!"

Riley forgot all about her lunch when she glanced outside to see a banged-up tour bus screeching to a halt outside the general store across the street, followed by a gray motorhome and an orange vintage muscle car.

Familiar faces jumped out of Keith's stolen black crew cab pickup, Shaun and Merle and Hayden running into the general store as Katanya and the two blonde siblings kept watch over the vehicles.

Passengers from the tour bus knocked confused pedestrians to the ground.

"Time to go," the man in the Hawaiian shirt decided, hauling his family out of the booth as he made a beeline towards the exit, knocking over the milkshakes in their haste.

"Hey, pay the bill, asshole!" Herb shuffled out from behind the counter as other customers began leaving the diner two by two.

"We should get going," Susan stood, stooping over her plate to take one more mouthful for the road, "Before they start turning on each other."

Riley was already halfway towards the front door, because among the crazed crowd running in and out of the town's general store, she had glimpsed a blob of blue and silver hurrying towards a stately white coupe.

CHAPTER 29

Riley shoved the diner's door open, the bell chiming its cheery farewell as she drew Clarence's pistol from the small of her back.

She narrowed her eyes at Stuart Sinclair, the chubby silver-haired doctor bustling towards his white coupe with an armful of supplies.

He was glancing back at the town's general store to make sure that he wasn't being followed, but he was looking in the wrong direction.

Icy adrenaline spiked Riley's heart rate as she flipped the safety lever off.

Drawing herself into a fighter's stance, she turned at the torso, cupping the bottom of her right hand and the pistol's hilt with her left.

She had Sinclair lined up in her sights while he fumbled with the car keys, dropping them by the driver's side door while Karen screamed at him from the passenger seat.

CRACK!

The bullet veered off course, shattering the rear window of the coupe.

Stuart bent over to pick up his keys before looking around.

His eyes went wide as he recognized Riley across the street, lining up her next shot.

She had her finger on the trigger again when her arm was knocked skywards, firing impotently up at the gray clouds.

"What are you thinking!?" Keith Bowman appeared beside her, his jaw set as he wrenched the gun out of her grip. "You could kill somebody!"

"Yeah, that's the plan," she nodded towards Sinclair as he started up the coupe.

"You don't even know how to aim yet," he whipped up the pistol, exhaled, and took a shot of his own at the coupe, leaving the side mirror dangling as Sinclair peeled off down Main Street. Keith flipped the safety lever on and straightened up, staring hard at Riley. "You could've killed somebody else. Somebody innocent. You don't want that on your conscience."

Riley was about to argue when more gunshots rang out across the street, as if they had given permission for everyone else to start shooting.

A man with two armfuls of canned goods rushed out of the general store, looking both ways before crossing the street. He made it two steps off the curb before the front of his shirt billowed out with red mist, the looter folding over and crumpling to the ground with his haul rolling away from him.

"That fat fuck with all the water just took off!" Shaun yelled, the barrel of his pistol smoking as he stared up the street. "Get the cans and let's move!"

Hayden obliged, running into the street to snatch up the spoils.

A mud-bellied pickup's wheels screeched as the woman garbed in camouflage hunting gear swerved to avoid him, plowing straight into the rigid front of an old farm truck.

It didn't matter whether the asteroid was a real threat or not – the people who still believed that it was coming were enough of a threat to society, their panic spreading like a disease to the peaceful small town.

"Where's Mom and Jesse?" Riley glanced at their old rust-bucket sedan as more gunshots erupted from the general store. "We have to go after Sinclair!"

"They're still inside," Keith grabbed her arm and swung her around, putting himself between her and the gunshots barking across the street as they ducked back into the diner, the bell above the door chiming its welcome.

"You best drop that peashooter, friend," Herb cocked a shot-gun behind the counter, pointing his double-barrel squarely at Keith's chest.

CHAPTER 30

"I'm a police officer!" Keith Bowman slowly raised his hands in the air beside Riley in the doorway of the diner, holding up the hilt of the pistol non-threateningly with the crook of his thumb. "I can help you defend this place."

"Bullshit, asshole," Herb snorted over the sound of the whimpering waitresses crouching behind the counter while bullets blasted across the street. He shifted his shotgun's barrels slightly as he glanced at the chaos spilling out of the general store, "Where's your badge?"

Keith glanced down at his waist, his pupils dilating as he remembered that he had surrendered his police kit belt to Shaun and the carjackers on the freeway.

"I don't have it on me," he confessed, glancing at Susan and Jesse on the far side of the diner, both of them ducking underneath the windowsill in the corner booth.

"I'll bet you never did – now drop the gun," Herb followed Keith with the shotgun as he slowly laid the pistol on the floor. "Mighty fine coincidence you and yours showed up on the same day this quiet little town went to hell."

"We're not with them," Riley spoke up, earning herself the

double-barrel's spotlight. Her voice quavered as she added, "It's the asteroid that's got everybody going crazy."

"Sure looked like you knew 'em," Herb narrowed his eyes at her, shifting the shotgun between the two of them, "Or y'all just shoot up strangers for fun?"

"He killed my dad," Riley fumed, only digging themselves deeper as she realized just how bad things must have looked.

Think real hard before you pull the trigger, Keith's voice echoed in her head.

"Listen up, Herb," Keith began in a measured tone, slowly lowering his hands to hook his thumbs through his belt loops, regaining his authority even while staring down the double-barrel shotgun, "Here's how this is gonna go – we're gonna get our people, and my handgun, and then we're getting outta here."

"Nobody has to get hurt," Riley drew strength from the assertive tone in his voice, "Mom, Jesse, come on, let's go."

"Y'all ain't getting off that easy," Herb swung his shotgun towards Susan and Jesse as they crawled out of the corner booth, bullets and screams still ringing across the street. "This is my town, and somebody's gonna be held accountable. Y'all are strangers, and so are 'em people outside. Now, you can either get a face full of buckshot, or, you can sit down, shut up, and finish your damn food while we wait for the sheriff and his deputies to sort all this shit out."

"I'm no stranger to Clementine," Susan found her voice as Riley and Keith joined her and Jesse on the other side of the diner. "I grew up an hour away from here. You might know my ma, Eleanor Tipton, or my sister, Lorraine."

"Lorraine Tipton," Herb echoed in recognition, still holding the double-barrel on them as he glanced down at the waitresses crouching behind the counter. "How can I forget *that* woman? She complains about the food every time she's in here until she gets a discount."

"So you know I'm a local," Susan folded her arms, standing in between Riley and Keith as Jesse hungrily returned to his meal. "What my daughter said was true. That man, Stuart Sinclair, shot and killed my husband while we were on the way here from Redhurst, California. This is my husband's partner on the force, Keith Bowman, and his son, Jesse."

"Y'all came a long way to stop just short of where you're going," Herb lowered his shotgun, but not his suspicious eyebrow. "Why are y'all here?"

"We ran into some bad people on the road," Keith explained, glancing out the window as the looters spread out from the empty shelves of the general store, targeting other businesses up and down Main Street instead. "My son needs a doctor."

"Alright then," Herb conceded with a heavy sigh, "Y'all help us get thr—"

The small bell above the diner's entrance chimed as the door slammed open, a pair of breathless desperados bursting through.

One was dressed in a sweat-stained singlet and sagging shorts. Tattoos covered both of his arms, from shoulder to wrist, along with a spider web across his neck and a black teardrop beneath one of his eyes.

The woman panting behind him had a scar across her cheek. Her hair was a tangled mess of black and gray. Her edgy eyes darted between Herb and the four in the far corner of the diner as her switchblade shook in her hand. The knife's edge dripped with fresh pearls of blood.

Riley recognized both of them – they were the same pair of

lowlifes who had tried to steal their supplies back at the rest stop in California.

The tattooed man was sizing up everyone in the diner before he caught Keith's eye, staring at the pistol on the floor at his feet.

A smile crept across his face, his silver tooth glinting between his scruffy mustache and beard.

Before he could bend down, the scar-cheeked woman pushed her partner aside as she dashed across the diner to leap over the counter.

Herb's shotgun jerked up and blasted her in the shoulder.

She shrieked in pain, but it didn't slow her down.

Before he could take another shot, she ducked underneath the double-barrel and knocked it to the floor as the screaming waitresses ran into the back.

In the same instant, the silver-toothed man snatched up the pistol, but Keith was on him before he could swing the gun up.

They rammed their shoulders together, doing a deadly dance around the weapon as stray slugs punched holes into the floor around their feet.

Herb was sprawled on his back across the counter, struggling with the scar-cheeked woman as she thrust all of her weight behind the switchblade, intent on sinking it into his chest.

Riley whirled around to grab the closest thing to hand – a salt shaker – and hurled it at the deranged woman.

The projectile missed, exploding a row of ceramic mugs hanging from a rack on the wall.

Susan grabbed her daughter's elbow, trying to hold her back, but Riley wrenched free of her grip and jumped behind the counter as Herb began to lose the fight, his shoes stumbling over his shotgun on the floor.

The woman snarled in exasperation, one of her arms dangling lamely from her wounded shoulder. She kicked one foot back against the wall for extra leverage over Herb, the tip of her switchblade inching closer to his chest.

"Hey, bitch!" Riley yelled, hooking her fingers through the handle of a coffee pot.

The scar-cheeked woman shot her an angry glare, just in time to receive a face full of shattered glass and scalding hot coffee.

The woman staggered backwards, screaming in agony, stabbing and slashing blindly as she retreated.

Breathing hard, Herb grabbed a bottle of liquor off the top shelf, lobbing it with the force of an amateur baseball pitcher directly at the woman's forehead.

One strike and she was out, falling backwards and cracking the back of her neck on the counter, her face still bubbling and blistering from the steaming coffee.

Riley dropped what was left of the coffee pot and ducked down to snatch up the shotgun, icy adrenaline drowning out the pain in her lower back.

The weapon was unwieldy compared to the pistol that she had practiced with, but she had to make do with what she had.

She swung the double-barrel up, looking for Keith and the tattooed man, but they had disappeared from view.

Leaning over the counter, she found three bodies tangled up on the floor.

Keith extracted himself from the knot, scrambling backwards to the pistol lying a few feet away.

He didn't bother raising the gun though – there was no need.

He wiped his mouth with the back of his hand, eyes wide and staring.

Tremors of impact shook Susan's arm as she plunged a steak knife in and out of the spider web tattooed across the looter's throat.

His lifeless body jolted with each thrust as his mouthful of blood obscured the gleam of his silver tooth.

"Mom?" Riley carefully set the shotgun down on the counter. "It's over. He's dead."

"Just making sure," her mother panted, setting aside the knife and looking back at Keith. "We should've taken care of them back at that rest stop. Who knows how many people they've killed since then?"

"Should've done a lot of things," Keith flipped the safety lever on the pistol.

Just as they were breathing a collective sigh of relief, a set of cutlery clattered to the floor in the back of the diner, and Jesse lurched over to one side.

CHAPTER 31

"Jesse, you okay!?" Keith crossed the distance of the diner in an instant. "Were you hit?"

"I don't feel so good," Jesse's head hung over the side of the bench, his mouth wide open as he sucked in shallow lungfuls of air.

"That's because you ate everybody's food," Keith relaxed with a chuckle, surveying the table. "Come on, sit up, you're making it worse."

"Middle of a fight and all he does is eat," Riley shook her head as she stepped over the dead woman, the scar on her cheek having spread across her entire face in the wake of the smashed coffee pot.

"I told you I was hungry," Jesse noisily suppressed a gag as he sat upright, queasily swaying on the bench.

The banged-up tour bus parked outside the general store across the street sped off as the gunfire died down.

Confused townsfolk shakily emerged from their hiding places to survey the damage, some of them stooping over the fallen bodies in the street to subtly scavenge whatever was left.

"We should get going," Susan made her way around the

diner's counter to wash the blood off her hands in the sink.

"Sure y'all don't wanna stick around?" Herb huffed as he dragged the dead woman out beside her partner. He leaned one of his hairy arms on the counter, still catching his breath. "If there's more where they came from, I could use a couple extra hands to help me circle the wagons. Free food and a room upstairs while you're here."

"We have somewhere else to be," Riley moved towards the window.

The orange vintage muscle car was gone, along with Keith's stolen black crew cab pickup.

Wherever Shaun and the other carjackers were heading, it seemed that they were traveling together with Sinclair.

"Well, hold on," Keith sat down opposite Jesse, considering Herb's offer. "This is a good spot here. Seems like a close community. If everybody works together, maybe we could fortify it, hold off any other attacks. Besides, we don't know if your relatives have enough food to feed the four of us. And we still need to find a doctor for Jesse."

"Stuart's a doctor," Jesse mumbled, staring down at the table as he remembered just how little he meant to the man.

"Yeah, a titty doctor," Keith snorted before looking around at them all. "What, you didn't know? Old Limp Dick's a plastic surgeon. The best thing he can do for anyone is make the Whore Queen less of an eyesore."

"Dad," Jesse scowled, reminding Keith that Karen was still his mother.

"What I don't get," Susan frowned as she shut off the sink's faucet and dried her hands on a dishcloth, "Is what they were doing all the way out here? I mean sure, they might've made it outta California, but why wouldn't they just stay on the

171

freeway? There's nothing out here for miles."

"Well, there's the camping trails, for one," Herb blustered, taking offense. "I thought you were a loc—"

"She didn't mean it like that," Riley cut across him, gritting her teeth as she gazed at her mother. "Back when we were leaving Redhurst, Dad gave Sinclair the farm's address, just in case we got split up along the way."

"Why would he do that!?" Susan stared back at her in disbelief.

"Dad made a deal for the water," Riley looked away, wondering just how differently things might have turned out if she and her father had managed to save one of the other two shopping carts full of water back at the supermarket.

"Doesn't sound like it was the only deal Old Limp Dick cut," Keith recalled Shaun's shout after Sinclair's coupe took off down the road. "He's working with the carjackers, maybe even the rest of the looters that just hit this town. Son of a bitch probably thinks your family has enough food for all of them on the farm."

"Well, what are we waiting for?" Susan crossed the diner towards the door, the bell chiming its farewell. She turned back to see that only Riley had moved to follow her outside. "Keith? Jesse? Are you coming?"

"Sorry, Susan, Riley," Keith couldn't bring himself to look either one of them in the eye. He sucked his front teeth and stared out the window at the overcast sky. "I gotta do what's best for my boy."

"But we *need* you," Susan pleaded from the door. "Keith, they're gonna kill my family!"

Herb quietly plucked his shotgun off the counter before slinking into the back with a guilty expression, realizing that his offer of free food and accommodation had been the reason why Keith was tempted to stay.

"Dad, we have to help them," Jesse's conscience compelled him to stand.

"There's no reason for us to die too," Keith reached across the booth and pinned Jesse's arm to the table, preventing him from trying to leave. "We don't have enough guns."

"Well, you've got one less now," Riley had heard enough.

She strode the length of the diner, snatched the pistol up off the table and slid it into the waistband of her jeans at the small of her back.

"You don't have to do this," Keith's jaw was set stubbornly as she stooped to pick up the bloody steak knife beside the pair of bodies. "You can stay here with us. We'll be alright here."

"You know, I used to think you were my uncle," Riley said in a choked voice as she handed the steak knife to her mother. She kept her back turned on him. She didn't want either of them to see her tears. "Back when I was a kid. And I thought Jesse was my cousin and Karen was my aunt. And why wouldn't you be family? We used to see each other every week, way more than we ever saw our *actual* relatives here in Nebraska."

"Riley, I'm –"

"But I was just a dumb kid," she turned around then, tears streaming down her face. She wanted them to see. "Just like that little boy in the monkey pajamas. Just a dumb kid. I hope every time you see him holding his stupid fucking airplane on the wrong side of the fence, you see the two of us standing right next to him."

CHAPTER 32

We're close, but we're not family, her mother's voice echoed in her head as the rolling fields and forests sailed by.

Riley Armstrong hadn't wanted to believe that Keith and Jesse would just leave her and Susan behind if the burden of staying together was too much for them to handle.

And in a way, they hadn't.

Riley and Susan were leaving them behind.

So why did it feel like they were the ones who had been abandoned?

"Take this shortcut," Susan pointed out an obscure dirt track between a thicket of green ash trees. "We might be able to get out in front of them."

The old rust-bucket sedan threatened to fall apart as Riley took the turn, the car's frame creaking and shuddering over every exposed root and rock.

Susan had made driving without the modern convenience of power steering seem easy, but Riley had to wrestle with the wheel just to keep the car straight.

Riley knew that she should have let her mother drive this last leg of the journey, but she had wanted to let off some steam in the driver's seat.

She hadn't even had enough time to check how many bullets were still in the pistol's magazine after Keith had wrestled it off the tattooed looter.

Riley was just about to pull over and let her mother take the wheel, when she glimpsed a break in the trees up ahead.

She recognized this patch of woods.

The rutted path that broke off to the left led down to a camping spot that her father had sometimes brought her to – whenever Aunt Lorraine's incessant needling would become too much for him.

She knew this part of Nebraska.

She could drive all the way to Grandma Eleanor's farm from here.

"How much time did we just save?" Riley glanced from side to side as they pulled out onto the highway again.

"Not enough," Susan sighed, pursing her lips. "We shouldn't have stopped to rest last night. We could've cut straight through Clementine and avoided the diner altogether. Maybe then, we wouldn't have split up."

"They made their choice," Riley narrowed her eyes at the road ahead as she stomped on the gas. "Fuck them."

"It was the smart choice," Susan ignored her daughter's profanity. Given that they had just racked up five kills on their body count over the past twenty-four hours, it was a little illogical to shelter her from the world by policing her language now. "I would've done the exact same thing if we were in their position."

"And I would've talked you out of it," Riley exhaled as they sped past a green mailbox that leaned closer to the ground with every year.

They were less than ten minutes away now.

"We don't even know what's waiting for us when we get there," Susan folded her arms, staring out the window. Not a moment later, she sat up in the passenger seat, peering at something in the distance. "Hey, slow down, do you see that?"

Riley saw it, but she had no intentions of slowing down.

A man with a tire iron was chasing a pair of backpackers down the side of the road.

Hearing the decrepit old sedan's engine, the two strangers stopped and waved their arms at the car, begging for them to pull over.

"Riley, we should help them," Susan turned her head as they flashed past. "Riley?"

"Not our people, not our problem," she finally saw the sense in the phrase, now more than ever. "Maybe they stole from that man. Maybe it's a trick, and they're all bad. I'm not risking getting carjacked again. Not when we're this close."

Even as the words left her mouth, she began to have second thoughts.

If those people had genuinely been calling out for help, she could have saved two lives, and in exchange, they might have been able to support Riley and Susan in the fight to come.

But then again, if the pair of them couldn't even protect themselves from one man with a tire iron, they wouldn't be much use in a shootout.

They were dead weight.

She kept her eyes on the road, determined not to look up at the rearview mirror.

"Turn around," Susan murmured after a few minutes of silence.

"You wanna save those people?" Riley kept her foot on the

gas, glancing sidelong at her mother.

"No, Keith's right," Susan conceded, shaking her head, wishing that he was wrong. "It's not safe for us. There's no reason for us to die too. We're alive. We've got each other."

"But we're almost there!" Riley was glad that she was driving now. "What about Grandma and Aunt Lorraine?"

"You're not doing this for them," Susan could tell by the determination on her daughter's face. "Riley, I want Sinclair dead as much as you do, but we only have one gun. You had your chance for revenge back in town. And we might get another chance one day. But if we rush into this now, we could get ourselves killed."

Riley pulled over onto the gravel shoulder.

Between the trees standing along the nature strip on the other side of the highway, they could see the dirt road leading to Grandma Eleanor's farm just up ahead.

If her grandmother was baking a pie, they were close enough to smell it on the breeze.

And if Sinclair and the carjackers had already reached the farm, it would have been the last pie that her grandmother would ever make.

"They didn't have guns before we came along," Riley furrowed her eyebrows as a thought occurred to her.

"What are you talking about?" Susan gazed sidelong at her with a combination of curiosity and confusion on her face.

"On the freeway," Riley remembered Shaun's jagged piece of wood after the carjackers had attacked them with eggs on the windshield, "They stole Dad's pistol and the shotgun from Keith's truck. And Sinclair got his pistol back at the parking garage."

"So?" her mother frowned.

"So, they're probably just as good with guns as I am," Riley met her gaze. "If I can get close enough, we can take them out."

"And if they're faster than you on the draw?" Susan folded her arms, shaking her head. "No, that's a gamble I'm not willing to take. Turn around, Riley, please."

Take care of your mother, Nolan Armstrong's final words echoed in Riley's ears. *Stay safe. Get to Nebraska.*

They were already in Nebraska.

And she had taken care of her mother.

But Riley wasn't doing too well on staying safe.

As much as she wanted revenge on Sinclair, she felt compelled to honor her father's last wishes.

With a heavy sigh, Riley put her hands back on the steering wheel.

She signaled, looking up at the rearview mirror, when she saw a twinkle in the reflection.

It was the flash of a distant windshield catching the sun.

"What if we got out in front of them?" Riley wondered aloud as she pulled out onto the highway, drawing parallel with the driveway to stare down the length of the dirt road towards the farm.

The only vehicle parked outside her grandmother's house was Aunt Lorraine's blue farm truck.

She glanced sidelong at her mother.

"Lorraine has a hunting rifle," Susan murmured as she gazed out the window, rethinking the gamble now that the odds were turned in their favor. "We might be able to hold them off."

That was all the permission Riley needed.

She hit the gas, turning down the dirt road as the trees lining the driveway flashed past on either side.

The waters of the small reservoir twinkled on the paddock

in the distance as the pine forest reared up behind the big weatherboard home.

Riley pulled the old rust-bucket sedan to a stop beside the blue farm truck.

She reached over the center console into the glove box for the spare bullets.

They didn't have much time before the carjackers worked out which driveway belonged to the farm, but she could reload the pistol's magazine inside the house.

They climbed out of the car, hearing a steady *thock* coming from the backyard.

Aunt Lorraine was probably chopping up firewood on the tree stump beside the vegetable garden.

"We're just in time," Susan breathed a sigh of relief as they slammed the car doors shut.

Riley waved as the living room's curtain moved, her heart leaping at the thought of hugging her grandmother again.

One moment later, the screen door banged open, and Shaun sauntered out onto the veranda with her father's stolen pistol drawn.

CHAPTER 33

Shaun fired a warning shot into the air before pointing the pistol at Riley and Susan.

Their hearts were in their throats as they ducked behind Aunt Lorraine's blue farm truck.

"I see you made it off the freeway," his eyes flicked towards their old rust-bucket sedan with a smarmy grin, "Guess you had to downgrade though."

Riley bit her bottom lip and glanced sidelong at her mother.

Out of the corner of her eye, she noticed fresh sets of tire tracks in the grass snaking around the side of the house.

They were so obvious.

She mentally kicked herself for not seeing them sooner.

Blinded by her desire for revenge, they had jumped straight into quicksand, and now they were stuck without a rope.

Crouching in between the two parked vehicles, at least they could take cover behind the farm truck.

It would have been easy enough for them to slip back into their own car, but whether the decrepit old sedan's engine would actually start in time was another matter entirely.

"What did you do to my ma and sister?" Susan called out

from behind the farm truck's rear wheel.

"Why don't you come on out and let's talk?" Shaun invited them closer as the big weatherboard home's screen door swung open behind him.

Hayden and Katanya joined him on the veranda to crouch behind the wooden railing, one holding Keith's shotgun, the other holding Lorraine's hunting rifle.

"Sure, just drop your guns first," Riley rattled the pistol out from the small of her back, drawing strength from the knowledge that she held the power to kill a man in the palm of her hand.

Flipping the safety lever off, she peered up at the three of them through the windows of the truck's cabin.

They weren't nearly close enough for her to feel confident with lining up a shot, but at least they were bigger targets than the fence post that she had practiced on.

Fence posts don't shoot back though, she admitted to herself.

Gripping the pistol in both hands, Riley let out a shallow breath, allowing herself a moment of caution to think it through properly.

Even if they didn't see her taking aim, she'd only have one shot before they started returning fire.

She had to make it count.

Riley chanced another glance through the truck's windows just as Merle loped around the side of the house to investigate all the noise, holding a hatchet in his wiry hand.

Protected by their apparent alliance with the carjackers, Karen Sinclair followed in his wake, wearing a pair of gardening gloves and an oversized red plaid shirt.

"Is that my husband's shirt!?" Susan yelled as soon as she caught sight of the woman between the farm truck's wooden side rails. "How dare you!"

"He wasn't using it," Karen shrugged behind Merle, soiling the cloth as she put her gloved hands on her hips. She took Susan's fuming red face as an invitation to go on the offensive. "I'm well within my rights to do as I please with it after you *shot* at us, back at that parking garage, and *again* in that shitty little town! How dare *you!?*"

"Nolan's dead, you fucking whore!" Susan's knuckles turned white around the bloody steak knife in her fist as she joined Riley at the front end of the farm truck, not even bothering to crouch for cover.

Karen's jaw dropped, her entire demeanor changing as she shook her head in disbelief.

"Enough!" Shaun was fed up with the back and forth between the two women. He addressed Riley and Susan, "If either of you wanna see Eleanor and Lorraine again, put your hands up and surrender."

"Give us a second!" Susan ducked behind the truck's hood. She murmured to Riley, "He knows their names. They could still be alive."

"And if they're not?" Riley cocked her head, "If we give up, they'll kill us next."

"Just follow my lead," Susan swallowed before raising her hands above the hood, the blood-stained steak knife gleaming dully in the afternoon sun.

"What the hell are you doing?" Riley whispered, glancing through the truck's cabin to see Shaun grinning on the veranda.

Flashbacks of the freeway and the shed in the woods strobed across her mind's eye.

Being stripped of their weapons and thrust down on their knees, held at the mercy of their captors. Lying face down on the musty moth-eaten mattress on the floor of the rusty old caravan.

She would rather die than let it happen again.

"Trust me," Susan urged, holding her daughter's gaze, "We're not giving them shit."

Still crouched behind the truck, Riley slowly held up her hands, her fingers wrapped tightly around the pistol's grip.

"Merle," Shaun called out to the gaunt middle-aged trucker standing beside the veranda, "Go relieve these ladies of their weapons. I guess the other two didn't make it?"

"What did you do to my Jesse?" Karen's shrill voice came from the side of the house, belatedly fearing the worst for her son, despite having abandoned him on the parking garage's roof.

"He was too weak to make the trip," Susan leaned against the truck's front quarter panel, nodding at Riley as Merle's footfalls drew closer. "We had to leave him behind. But you know what that's like, don't you?"

A second pair of footfalls came running, and an instant later, Karen appeared, her haughty face livid.

"You tell me where he is," she snarled as she seized Susan's knife hand, tugging the blade free with her gardening gloves, "Right now."

"Hold on a second," Merle loped around the front of the truck. His eyes flicked from Susan to Riley. "Drop the gun."

"I only need one of you to tell me what happened to my son," Karen flipped the steak knife and held it to Susan's throat, daring Riley to give her a reason to slice.

With her hands still raised, pistol in the air, Riley glanced sidelong at her mother.

The blade scratched Susan's throat as she gulped nervously.

183

Merle bounced the weight of the hatchet in his hand, his patience wearing thin.

"You know what I love about that shirt?" Susan stared pointedly at Karen's oversized red plaid top. "It won't matter if you bleed on it – RILEY, NOW!!"

Icy adrenaline pumped through Riley's veins.

She ducked underneath Merle's axe swing, the hatchet's head burying into the truck's front quarter panel.

His pupils dilated as he stared down the barrel of her pistol.

CRACK!

Merle's head snapped backwards, blood mist spraying the side of the old rust-bucket sedan as he fell to his knees, his gaunt face contorted around the third hole in his nose.

Susan and Karen were rolling across the grass, wrestling for control of the steak knife.

Riley turned the pistol on them, finger off the trigger, waiting for the Whore Queen to rear her ugly head.

Click.

Riley squeezed the trigger again, only for it to give another impotent *click.*

She turned the gun in her hands.

The slide was cocked back.

The chamber was empty.

"Shit," she breathed, the box of spare bullets bulging in her front pocket.

There was no time to reload.

Karen was on top of her mother.

Susan had managed to get the steak knife in her hands, but Karen was turning the blade back towards her chest.

Riley sprang forward, slamming the handgun's hilt into Karen's temple, knocking her sideways.

Susan quickly recovered and rolled over, the steak knife poised in her fist, ready to go to work.

"Susan, stop!" Karen's eyes were wide with terror, lying on her back, holding up her hands in surrender. "Please, we were friends once, weren't we?"

"Our husbands were friends," Susan's scathing voice dripped between her gritted teeth, knowing that Karen wouldn't have shown her a shred of mercy, "Up until your new husband killed mine."

She plunged the blade into Karen's stomach, flecks of blood spurting as she pulled the knife out to stab her again.

Riley's fingers shook as she fumbled the box of bullets from her front pocket, her eyes transfixed on her mother giving herself over to her rage and fury.

"Help me!" Karen shrieked up at the sky as she feebly flailed her arms to block the blade, catching hold of Susan's wrist with her gloved hands in a last ditch effort to cling to life. Karen glanced sidelong at Riley before screaming again, "She's reloading!"

Rocking forward on her knees, Riley pistol-whipped Karen in the mouth, knocking her bleached front teeth down her throat.

Karen's hands instinctively flew up to shield her face as she coughed and gagged on her own teeth, freeing Susan to resume.

Quickly looking away, Riley's fingers scrabbled over the side of the pistol's grip, searching for the magazine release.

She hadn't been shown how to reload a gun, but she knew that there was a button or a switch or *something* that would drop the empty magazine.

Just a few feet away, Susan was shanking and slashing Karen's torso, the sickening squelches providing her a catharsis from all of the chaos that had turned their world upside down over the past few days, ruining Nolan Armstrong's red plaid shirt beyond recognition.

"Fuck me," somebody croaked behind them as a shotgun's shell cocked into the breech.

CHAPTER 34

"Somebody get the doctor!" Hayden yelled over his shoulder, stifling a gag as he held Riley and Susan at gunpoint with Keith's stolen shotgun.

"Don't bother, they're already dead," Katanya appeared around the other side of the blue farm truck, wearing Riley's clothes and carrying Aunt Lorraine's hunting rifle. With a grim expression, she jerked the rifle's barrel at the mother and daughter kneeling beside the bodies on the blood-slick grass, "Move. Now."

Riley and Susan were caught in between the two carjackers.

There was no way that they could make a play for either one of the guns without getting shot in the back. Whether Hayden and Katanya were gun novices or trained professionals, it didn't matter at this distance.

Dropping the empty pistol and the bloody steak knife, Riley and Susan rose to their feet, stepping away from the grisly scene.

"Hey, Doc!" Shaun shouted as they emerged from between the two vehicles. "Gonna need you out here."

There was movement in the living room's window, Stuart

Sinclair's mop of silver hair drooping low over his forehead as he timidly peered out from behind one of the curtains.

On the other side of the living room, the two blonde siblings were keeping watch over Grandma Eleanor and Aunt Lorraine.

At least they're still alive, Riley thought to herself, although she didn't like their chances of staying that way now.

"I guess you want us on our knees," Susan supposed in a quiet voice, having spent all of her aggression on butchering Karen.

"Kneel, sit, stand," Katanya shrugged, keeping a wary eye on them from a few yards away. "Hold a yoga stretch – I don't give a shit. Just don't move."

Riley stood, as did her mother.

"You know, I really should be thanking you," Shaun began, sitting down on the veranda's steps, "We wouldn't have made it this far without your gas, your guns, your grub. I'll bet you brought even more with you. Hayden, go check their trunk, see what they've got for us."

The shotgun rattled as Hayden's footfalls faded in the direction of the old rust-bucket sedan.

"Looks like they came through for us again," he reported as the trunk's hatch creaked open, rifling through the grocery bags. "Even got some chocolate back here."

"Throw me one," Shaun caught the purple bar with one hand, setting his pistol down to unwrap it.

"I hope you get a fucking toothache, prick," Riley resented his groan of satisfaction.

"Good thing you packed your toothbrush," he winked, happily chewing his mouthful.

"Where's Karen?" Sinclair pushed the screen door open, gazing around the front yard before his eyes fixated on the fresh blood spattered up Susan's forearms. "You... what have you done?"

"You killed my husband," Susan put one hand on her hip with a contented smile, staining the side of her shirt red. "So I killed your wife."

Hayden nodded gravely at Stuart as he climbed up the veranda's stairs, one hand holding the shotgun by the barrel, the other carrying the grocery bags as he headed inside.

"But your husband was still alive!" Sinclair clapped a meaty hand to his mouth, staring in disbelief at Shaun and Katanya, putting on an act of innocence for his companions, as if he was on trial. "It wasn't – I – I couldn't possibly... It was self defense, you see? But you..." his trembling fingers drew Keith's stolen handgun from the front pocket of his tracksuit pants, whipping the barrel up at Susan, "You killed Karen, you murderer!"

Riley hugged her mother, putting herself in the line of fire.

"Move aside!" Stuart fumed, the pistol rattling in his shaky grip.

"Go ahead, shoot me in the back," Riley dared him. If she and her mother were going to die anyway, she wanted to do it on her terms, "Just like you shot my dad in the back."

"We're coming, Nolan," Susan whispered into her daughter's ear.

Katanya's hard gaze softened as she stared at the tears welling in Riley's eyes.

Riley and Susan waited for the shot, but it never came.

Still embracing each other, they slowly turned back towards the veranda.

"Hold on a second, Doc," Shaun was still lounging on the veranda's stairs, but he had one hand on Sinclair's arm. Shaun lowered the pistol as he tossed his empty chocolate wrapper aside. "They just did us a favor."

"They killed my wife!" Stuart turned a shade of red, glaring down at Shaun.

"And Merle," Katanya added as Riley and Susan broke apart to watch them argue.

"Yeah, you're forgetting one thing though," Shaun dusted his hands and grabbed his pistol off the veranda, standing face to face with Sinclair. "You said there was gonna be plenty of food here. Enough for all of us."

"What does that have to do with these two murderers!?" Sinclair straightened up his jacket with a huff.

"Pantry's average," Shaun continued, walking down the stairs with his arms out wide, "Basement's full of wine. Vegetable garden might hold us over – for a week or two. I think we brought more food with us than what they have to offer. You promised there would be enough to pass around for a year."

"They're holding out on us!" Sinclair waggled one of his fat sausage fingers in the air, "There's a storm shelter around here somewhere. I know it! But they don't respect you. They need to be shown who's boss. Starting with these two."

Riley stared daggers at Sinclair as he pointed in their direction.

"You know, I couldn't agree more," Shaun grinned, standing to one side, his gaze going from Stuart on the veranda to Riley and Susan in the yard. "I was actually considering letting you two live – you're resourceful. We might have been able to work together... But you've shown me another way."

Riley furrowed her eyebrows, exchanging a confused glance with her mother.

"Less mouths, more food," he explained as Hayden reappeared in the mesh of the screen door. Shaun looked up at

Sinclair. "What do you think? A life for a life seem fair? How about a two for one special?"

"What are you talking about, Shaun?" Katanya asked behind Riley and Susan. "You're not gonna kill two women, are you?"

"Four, actually," he corrected her, frowning and smiling at the same time, as if it was all so obvious. "These two just killed our people. And the ones in there have served their purpose." Shaun nodded towards Riley, "She shot our old person, so it's only right that we shoot theirs. Then I'll kill her, and Doc can have the other two."

"That's not cool, Shaun," Hayden pushed the screen door open. "That old lady said she was gonna make beds for all of us."

Riley could see them turning on each other, and her eyes went to her father's stolen pistol dangling in Shaun's hand, only a few yards away.

Her chances of wrestling the gun off him and taking them out were slim, but it was better than none at all.

She glanced sidelong at her mother, trying to get her attention.

"And then what?" Shaun cocked his head at Hayden, turning his back on Riley and Susan, "She'll be another mouth to feed. She's already got one foot in the grave anyway. Better to – what the fuck?"

A ball of white light sailed across the sky, blazing westward like a second sun, with a fiery tail glowing in its wake.

"There's the asteroid," Katanya shielded her eyes with one arm, frowning as she watched. "Hold on – does it look like it's turning?"

Riley couldn't care if the asteroid bounced off the lower layers of the atmosphere and flew back up into space.

This was their chance.

Cold adrenaline shooting through her veins, she lunged for the pistol in Shaun's grip, grabbing the barrel with one hand and twisting his wrist with the other.

Behind her, a wooden clack and rattle sounded as Susan latched onto the hunting rifle, pulling Katanya's focus back to earth as they wrestled for the weapon.

"Get off me!" Shaun snarled, throwing his weight into Riley, knocking her off balance as they both fell to the ground. "Hayden, Doc, kill them!"

"I can't get a clear shot!" Hayden yelled from the veranda, Sinclair equally as hindered.

Riley dug her fingernails into Shaun's wrist, clawing and gouging at his skin, doing her best to keep the pistol's barrel pointing away from her.

BADOOM!!

Her heart froze, and she glanced over at her mother, still struggling with Katanya.

For a moment, it had sounded like a shotgun blast, but then they were hit with the roar of rolling thunder as the sonic boom of the asteroid reached them.

Shaun snapped his jaws at Riley, madness emanating from the crazed gleam in his eyes.

Maybe it had been born from the chaos over the past few days.

Maybe it had always been there, lying dormant, waiting for an excuse to surface.

Wherever his frenzied insanity had come from, he was beginning to gain the upper hand, his murderous intent edging closer to Riley with every passing moment.

Fighting to keep the gun in the air, she jerked her face away from his foaming teeth, kneeing him in the groin.

He didn't budge.

He didn't even wince.

If anything, the pain only made him stronger, and he slowly began turning the barrel towards her midsection.

GUVV!!

The hunting rifle woofed a finger of hot lead, ripping through flesh.

"Riley!?" Susan screamed from somewhere far away, all the sound sucked out of the air.

Warm blood splashed across her face, Riley didn't glance over at her mother this time.

Her eyes were transfixed on the sight of Shaun's snapping teeth, still working towards her even as blood gushed out of his jugular vein, his hands turning limp around the pistol.

One down, three to go, Riley's senses flooded back to her, and she jerked the gun out of Shaun's lifeless fingers.

She turned the gun on Hayden first, but he had already dropped the shotgun, running down the veranda's steps towards his fallen friend.

Katanya had her hands up, shaking her head in surrender, backing away from Susan as she held the smoking hunting rifle.

"Drop the fucking gun!" Riley shouted at Sinclair as she sidestepped away from Hayden and Shaun.

Stuart's hands trembled, caught in the sights of both women who had every right and reason to paint the veranda with his blood.

The pistol in his clammy grip was rattling so violently, he wouldn't have been able to hit either one of them even if he tried.

"P–please," he dropped the gun and fell to his knees on the veranda. "I never meant to kill Nolan. You have to believe me.

We weren't even supposed to be up there. It was all Keith's fault!"

"It doesn't matter whose fault it was," Riley marched up the stairs as the sky flashed and the ground rumbled. She ignored the gasps behind her as she kicked Sinclair's pistol across the veranda's wooden floor. "You killed my dad."

"Don't do this!" Stuart's bottom lip quavered as he begged and bargained for his life, gazing up at Riley's blood-spattered face. "I'm – I'm a doctor!" he faltered, distracted by something over her shoulder. "The whole world's about to change, and you're gonna need my help. Just look!"

He waggled one of his fat sausage fingers past her hip, but she knocked his arm aside, knowing that he was probably just trying to feed her the same bullshit that he had given the carjackers.

"Keith told us what kinda doctor you are," she thrust her pistol into his face and grabbed a handful of his silver hair, only for the wig to peel off his scalp, revealing a giant bald patch. She tossed his wig aside with a snort, "We don't need plastic surgeons in the apocalypse... Like it would've made any difference."

Riley seized him by the throat and shoved him back against the wall, savoring the fear scrawled across his face as she stared into his wide eyes.

She traced her father's pistol around to the side of his head, committing the sight of Stuart Sinclair's pathetic pleas to memory before squeezing the trigger.

His eyes glassed over as his brain fired the final synapses of despair, and she threw his lifeless body to the floor.

Riley stood upright with a contented sigh, the burden of her vengeance lifting as a tide of relief washed over her.

There was movement in the living room window again

as Aunt Lorraine gazed out through the glass, the pair of blonde siblings standing on either side, equally hypnotized by something in the distance.

Riley turned then.

A gray motorhome was pulling into the driveway, but that wasn't what everyone was staring at.

Rising silently on the horizon was a haze of ash.

Mushroom clouds were reaching up into the sky.

Half a dozen of them.

CHAPTER 35

The gray motorhome trundled down the driveway, with Jesse Bowman behind the wheel. Keith leapt out from the passenger side while the vehicle was still rolling, swinging the butt of a double-barrel shotgun up to his shoulder.

"Hands where I can see them!" Keith swept the shotgun from Katanya to Hayden. "Susan, Riley, everything okay?"

"You're a little late," Susan held the hunting rifle pointed at the ground. She glanced at the double-barrel on his shoulder. "Where'd you get the gun?"

"Borrowed it," Keith circled around Hayden kneeling on the ground, stifling a snort at the sight of Shaun bleeding out, "Would've come earlier, but that asshole back at the diner made us pay for lunch." He nodded up at Riley standing on the veranda, "We had to come though. You're our people. You're our family."

"Mom!?" Jesse threw the driver's side door open and ran across the yard.

"Don't," Katanya caught him in the crook of her elbow, trying to hold him back.

"Get off me!" Jesse shoved her aside, disappearing behind

the blue farm truck.

"We had to," Susan swallowed, her voice quieting as she averted her gaze. "I had to."

Keith shrugged his indifference, but he winced at the sound of his son wailing in anguish.

Riley was still staring at the mushroom clouds rising up on the horizon when the screen door swung open behind her.

She turned to see her grandmother smiling.

"Oh, Riley, it's good to see you again," Grandma Eleanor doddered forward with her arms open, before noticing Sinclair slumped over to the side, and Shaun's body lying on the grass. She took another look at Riley, filled with concern, "There's blood on your face, dear, are you hurt?"

"It's not mine," Riley awkwardly fell into her grandmother's embrace with one arm, her other hand still holding her father's pistol.

"Good, that's good, that's all that matters," Eleanor Tipton cooed, finding a clean patch of skin to plant a soft kiss on her cheek. "Your friends said you were coming. I think they ruined the surprise, but I'm happy you're here."

"Ma?" Susan almost couldn't believe her eyes. She rested the hunting rifle against the wall before staggering up the steps, wrapping her arms around her mother. Tears welled in her eyes, "There were so many times I didn't think we'd ever see you again."

"Oh hush, child, I haven't kicked the bucket yet," Grandma Eleanor swelled in defiance despite her old age. She drew back, peering at Keith standing in the yard. "Where's Nolan?"

Susan shook her head as her tears fell, feeling like a little girl in her mother's arms again.

"What should we do with these two?" Keith broke in, nodding

towards Hayden and Katanya.

Unarmed, the pair of them didn't pose much of a threat, but he kept the shotgun trained on them all the same.

Hayden rubbed his cheeks as he and Katanya looked up from the grass, their lives hanging in the balance.

"We didn't want this," Katanya swallowed, holding her hands up. "We were just trying to defend ourselves."

"Shaun was my best friend," Hayden choked as he stepped away from the body in the grass. "He got us here, but somewhere along the way, he changed. We're not like him."

"It's true," Aunt Lorraine opened the screen door and stepped out onto the veranda, the pair of blonde siblings trailing out behind her. "These ones treated us well. We didn't even know anything was wrong until you showed up."

They all turned to Susan, and she turned to Riley.

Feeling the weight of everyone's stares, Riley climbed down the veranda's steps into the yard, hearing Jesse's strained sobs rising up from behind the blue farm truck.

Keith's grip on the double-barrel held steady as he waited for her to decide their fates.

Not our people, she began to think to herself. She gazed around at Katanya, Hayden, and the two blonde siblings quaking on the veranda. They were only a few years older than Riley. *But they could be.*

She gazed up at the mushroom clouds on the horizon again.

They had seen enough death for one day.

All of them had.

Her eyes fell to the treetops of the pine forest rearing up behind her grandmother's big weatherboard home.

"Mom?" Riley began as she slid her father's pistol into her waistband of her jeans at the small of her back. "Could you show me how to get the nuts out of a pinecone?"

* * *

Keep reading for an exclusive sneak peek at the next book –
Raiders of The Fall.

Find out what happens next!

Thank you so much for reading Survivors of The Fall. I hope you enjoyed the story.

I wrote an extra scene that didn't survive the final cut, but I've saved it for you!

Join my newsletter here to receive the free bonus epilogue – unavailable anywhere else.
https://BookHip.com/FVVTMAA

I'd also like to invite you to my Book Lovers Facebook Group. Chat with me, have a character named after you, talk with other fans, and win exclusive prizes and giveaways.
Join the fun!
www.facebook.com/groups/SteveHeuzinkveldVIPFans

Here's a QR code so you don't have to type out any links:

Keep turning the pages for a sneak peek at the next book –
Raiders of The Fall.
Or continue reading on Amazon:
www.amazon.com/dp/B0BQZ7VJMX

ACKNOWLEDGMENTS

First and foremost, I want to thank my beautiful wife, Hariezoy, for supporting me and encouraging me every single day, and for giving me the freedom to burn the midnight oil to hit the keyboard every night until the sun comes up.

We recently had a healthy baby boy, and she was an absolute superwoman during the entire birth. She didn't even make a sound, and I stood by the bed thinking of that one scene from A Quiet Place!

A huge thanks also goes to my Patreon followers, Greg Hyndman, Rupert Lugo, and Martin Georgiev. Your continued support has really helped soften the financial impact in hiring professional artists for my book covers, the ongoing website costs, and all of the other expenses that it takes to keep this author's dreams alive!

I'd like to thank the law enforcement officers of the AskLE SubReddit, and in particular, Apoplectic Ignoramous, for their expert insight into emergency services, and for the personal sacrifices that they make each and every day to keep our communities safe.

I also want to thank Adam Beswick and Inez Drapiewska, for their gems of wisdom and much appreciated advice in navigating the wild west of TikTok marketing. I'm still getting the hang of it, but if you've found this book through one of my videos, then it's working!

I'm going to give a shout-out to Daniel Burns too, for collecting every post-apoc book and posting them all in my favorite Facebook groups. He doesn't even know that I put him in here lol - let's see how long it takes for him to spot this and tag me!

And last but not least, thank you. As an independently-published author, this is very often a one-man show, and after the hours upon hours I've invested into this project, it means the world to me that you've taken the time to meet the characters living in my head.

I'd love to put your name here in my future books, right alongside Greg, Rupert and Martin. Join us on Patreon for access to never-before-seen chapters from my other works, as well as autographed copies of future books, all while helping me to bring more stories to life!

www.patreon.com/SteveHeuzinkveld

Be sure to follow me on Amazon to receive a notification when my next book releases!

www.amazon.com/Steve-Heuzinkveld/e/B09FZFK2XW

P.S. I love hearing from my fans - feel free to contact me any time!

   -Steve
author@SteveHeuzinkveld.com
www.SteveHeuzinkveld.com

Preview - Raiders of The Fall

"Who the hell could've done this?" Hayden Marsh put their thoughts into words, covering his nose with the collar of his undershirt as they crept through the eerie streets of the forever-silenced small town.

"I thought this place was supposed to be safe," Chelsea Preston shrank away from the bullet-riddled bodies strewn across the sidewalks, fighting the urge to gag.

"We should get back to the truck," Katanya Grady checked their rear with a sweep of her hunting rifle, making sure that their escape route was still clear. "Whoever did this might still be hanging around."

"I don't think so," Riley Armstrong held her father's pistol up as she led the way. "Whoever did this, it was a big group. We would've seen somebody by now."

Despite her confidence, Riley still stopped short of every store window and open door, glancing at the empty shelves and overturned offices inside before resuming their steady advance up Clementine's Main Street.

She stepped over a familiar dead body as they passed by a brick-lined bank.

It was the same greasy mechanic who would wolf-whistle at her every time they came into Clementine to trade.

The mechanic – along with countless others – had been running from whoever had stormed the town. Riley could tell by the bullet spray across the brick wall and the bloody streak that he had left along the pavement, crawling half a dozen yards towards whatever he thought could have saved him.

Evidently, he had thought wrong.

"Don't tell me we're still looking for batteries," Katanya spoke softly from the rear of their single file formation along the sidewalk.

"Where else are we gonna find them?" Riley glanced back at the other three. She jerked her head towards the town's main intersection, "Herb's diner's just up ahead. Let's head there first and then we'll check the store."

Pressing her shoulder into the bricks of a building, Riley scanned the corner on the other side of the street, checking for any signs of movement.

With her forefinger laid alongside her pistol's trigger guard, she swept the gun's barrel back across the road, before edging out from behind the corner.

Broken bottles and scorch marks blotched the intersection. Glass crystals twinkled in windswept piles underneath the shattered windows of the diner.

"Herb!" Riley called across the desolate street. She knew that she was giving away their position, but she'd rather have a shootout with hostiles before engaging in friendly fire. "We're coming over!"

She gazed back at her three companions with bated breaths, waiting for the man's neighborly acknowledgment that never came.

Herb was being cautious.

He had to be.

There was no doubt in her mind that the portly man was watching them from one of the second-story windows above the diner, with his double-barrel shotgun tracing their every move.

Ruddy streaks flowed down the diner's steps onto the pavement like a rusty red carpet that abruptly ended at the curb.

The front door had been kicked off the hinges, hanging ajar at an odd angle, solely suspended by a twisted scrap of metal in the doorway.

Riley peered inside through the broken entrance, with Hayden backing her up on the steps while Katanya and Chelsea warily glanced up and down the ghostly intersection.

Lead pellet craters pockmarked the diner's walls, surrounded by copper red sprays and splotches of blood. Spent shotgun shells and a windswept stack of table napkins littered the floor. Splintered strips of wood hung from the booths where bodies had fallen backwards onto the tables, although there were no signs of the raiders' carcasses now.

The small bell above the diner's entrance gave a mournful chime as Riley shouldered the stubborn door open, the hanging frame scraping noisily along the floor.

Behind the counter, surrounded by empty boxes of ammo, with one hand eternally reaching up for one of the few remaining bottles of liquor on the top shelf, Herb's body was draped unceremoniously over the sink with a hole in the back of his head.

Riley's pupils dilated at the sight of the slumped diner owner.

She had only known the man for a few months, but he had been the community's lifeblood – the reason why most of them had even lasted this long after the apocalypse.

And now he was dead, along with the rest of Clementine's

townsfolk.

"Check the back," she glanced sidelong at Hayden before walking the length of the diner, sweeping each booth to make sure that they were truly alone before jumping behind the counter.

With a strained grunt, Riley heaved Herb's body from the sink, sending his stiffened corpse to the floor with a hollow thud.

Swallowing the lump building in her throat, she rolled him onto his back with the heel of her sneaker and forced herself to look down.

Despite the violence of his death, the big friendly owner of the diner had died grinning. With windows shattering around him, bullets flying overhead and the raiders kicking down his door, Herb had been in the midst of his last stand, defending Clementine to his final breath.

Riley crouched beside him, her fingers moving to close his lifeless eyelids, when she drew her hand away, flinching at the thought of touching him, afraid that she would disturb his rest and contort his smiling face into something far more sinister.

"Looks like they cleaned house," Hayden emerged from the kitchen, stopping short of Riley and Herb as he surveyed the grisly scene behind the counter. "Place is empty."

"Did you check upstairs?" she peeled a sticky bar mat off the counter and knelt down again to lay it over Herb's head – hardly the shroud that the man deserved, but better than what he had been given.

"Yeah," Hayden frowned as he stared up at the bottles of liquor on the top shelf. "They even took the mattresses off the bed frames." He stepped over Herb's body to reach up for an expensive-looking bottle of bourbon before glancing back down at Riley. "Dunno how the hell they missed this though."

Riley cocked her head in contemplation, her gaze flicking over towards the other bottles remaining on the liquor rack, when a pair of footsteps scuffed across the pavement towards the diner's entrance.

* * *

Continue reading on Amazon:
www.amazon.com/dp/B0BQZ7VJMX

Made in the USA
Coppell, TX
26 July 2023

19629524R00125